ARCANE REVENANT

THE DARKLAND DRUIDS - BOOK FOUR

NICOLE R. TAYLOR

Arcane Revenant (The Darkland Druids - Book Four) by Nicole R. Taylor

Copyright © 2020 by Nicole R. Taylor

All rights reserved.

This book is written in British/AU English.

No part of this book may be reproduced in any form or by any electronic or mechanical means, including information storage and retrieval systems, without written permission from the author, except for the use of brief quotations in a book review.

www.nicolertaylorwrites.com

Cover Design: Pixie Covers & Nicole R. Taylor

Edited by: Silvia Curry

1

———

As it turned out, Sil Astrad was indeed a city of stars.

The stone walls of the capital rose into the cloudless sky, dwarfing everything within a hundred miles. Towers adorned with pointed flags—a shining eight-pointed silver star on a field of creamy white, edged with metallic gold—dotted along the structure and the same design flowed on either side of the approaching city gates.

Our group of riders followed the main road towards the enormous gates at the western entrance and my heart fluttered.

My grey horse flattened its ears at the commotion on the road and I had the same reaction. After spending weeks travelling, and another week in the mountain village of Un Alari, the hustle and bustle of a great city like the Fae capital threatened to send me running in the opposite direction. It had nothing to do with the fact that I would soon be standing before the Fae Queen, Niarisshia, as the *Liash li Ashli*—the goddess of death.

Actually, it was ninety-five percent to do with that.

I glanced at Rory, who rode beside me. He'd been here for a month and would know what to do, but we hadn't had a chance to talk yet. Altrys, the Fae *Shr'lei de Delei'an*—Blade of the Queen—who rode on my other side, had told me a few things but none of them helped to curb my anxiety.

I was the creature prophesied by the fanatic sect of Fae known as the Chimera to be the catalyst for their plan to remake the Fae world. My power would carry the unworthy into death, paving the way to their so-called 'golden age'. Whatever label they chose to put on it, it was genocide, and I wouldn't have any part of it, prophecy be damned.

As we approached Sil Astrad, my nerves turned into mush at the sight of the famed City of Stars. The walls glittered with quartz, and beyond, I could see the tip of a shining building on top of a rise, sparkling like a jewel plucked right out of the night sky.

"What's that building?" I asked Altrys. "The one on the hill."

"That's the palace," the *Shr'lei* replied, holding his arm across his chest to steady his injured shoulder. "The queen's residence."

"They call it Lor As'tuann," Rory told me.

I glanced at him, but he was looking past me at Altrys. He had a foul look on his face and I slapped his arm. The last thing I needed right now was a macho match between the two men. How I was going to tell Rory about Altrys and I was a problem I wanted to save for another day.

Rory opened his mouth to complain and I shook my head. His jaw snapped shut, but not before shooting Altrys another convoluted glare.

Elion, the *Shr'lei de Delei'an* who'd met Altrys and I on the road outside of Ad Valrah, was riding at the head of the group. As we approached the gate, he lifted his arm and gestured to the guards. The enormous steel doors opened and the column of soldiers moved through, sweeping us into the city.

I shivered as I rode underneath the arch. This place reverberated with energy, as if the stones were drenched with magic. Perhaps the literal meaning of 'City of Stars' would make itself known come nighttime.

We made quite the spectacle as we were escorted along a wide thoroughfare. Anyone who was on the road scurried to the side, allowing the soldiers to pass unhindered. Fae of all kinds gathered along the edges, watching the procession with mingled curiosity and awe.

I wasn't sure who they were staring at most. Me, who was the harbinger of death, Rory, the Druid from another world, or Ignis, the massive black and blue tiger made from foreign magic.

Never one for being the centre of attention, I held my head high and took in the city instead.

The stone buildings with the exposed wooden beams reminded me of Un Alari, but they were more polished. The roads were paved, the gardens were manicured, but the trees were left to grow unhindered, giving the streetscapes a forested feel. Birds played amongst the foliage and picked at moss dangling from gnarled branches

Strings of crystal lights hung across openings leading to twisting alleyways, colourful signs swung outside shops, and I caught glimpses of markets hidden amongst the patchwork of buildings.

The people were equally as vibrant as the city they inhabited. Shri'danann—Fae who were born with magic—mingled with the common De'ashlide, their coloured hair bright against the brown of their counterparts. Unlike Un Alari, the divide between the two was clearer in the capital.

Magic came with wealth and status and it showed in the clothes they wore, the shops they entered, and the way they stared at our procession as we passed. The De'ashlide had only a passing curiousness about what was going on. Some lingered to watch when they saw the soldiers, but most scurried away down the twisting alleys soon after.

We continued along the thoroughfare, approaching the silver gates of the palace. Guards dressed in fine armour rushed to open them, allowing us to pass unhindered. The perimeter vibrated as we rode through, and I glanced at the fence.

"Magic," Altrys told me. "The entire wall is imbued with power."

"It's an epic electric fence," Rory added.

I snorted. The wall had to be filled with the equivalent of a hundred thousand volts… *at least*. It was one hell of a security system.

Two finely dressed Fae waited for us in the courtyard, the white and silver palace towering behind them. As we dismounted, I managed to size them up.

Studying the gardens and mossy rocks was the least of my concerns. Un Alari was one thing, but this place…? I felt danger in the air, and it wasn't the kind I could fight with my knife.

I recognised Elmarrin, the Fae ambassador who'd come with me and Rory from Ireland. He looked dour and not pleased to see us at all. In the short time I'd spent with him, he'd proven to be arrogant and thoroughly annoying—an opinion shared by the Crescent Witches, the coven who guarded the Fae portal back on Earth.

No, I hadn't missed Elmarrin at all.

The other Fae was a woman. She was petite and her long hair was a pastel orange colour. Her form fitting dress matched, the fine fabric glittering with threads of gold. It flared out from her waist slightly, but it looked more like feminine armour than a gown to me.

Altrys waited, allowing Rory to escort me. I glanced at him and he nodded. He was supposed to be impartial, despite what had happened to us on the road.

"Welcome to Sil Astrad and the Lor As'tuann, Elspeth Odhweine," the woman said. "And welcome home, Altrys, *Shr'lei de Delei'an*." Her smile returned to me, her eyes burning with an odd light. "I am La'luin, *Li'deshri*. Mistress to the queen."

I hesitated. "Mistress?"

"Mistress means something else here," Rory murmured and turned to the woman. "It's nice to see you again, La'luin."

She smiled. "I saw you this morning, Raurich."

"And it's always a pleasure."

I stifled a groan. Rory hadn't been idle since I'd been away. He'd brought out his Scottish rogue persona to woo the womenfolk. Ignis leaned against my leg and I had the feeling the Druid had been using the tiger as his wingman.

"Elion, *Shr'lei de Delei'an*," La'luin said, turning to the older warrior, "Ilbryen awaits your arrival in the citadel. Altrys, the queen bids you to visit the healers at once. Your report will wait until after." I tried to follow the commands, but she spoke them so quickly, it sounded like gibberish to me. "Elspeth, Raurich," she looked down at Ignis and a strange look passed across her features, "and your tiger, please follow me."

I looked to Altrys, not expecting to be parted from him so soon.

"All is well," he told me. "When I have seen to these formalities, I will find you."

As I watched the men walk away, La'luin beckoned for us to follow her.

Ignis happily trotted before our little group, relishing the looks the guards gave him as they opened the doors to the palace.

"Nothing to say, Elmarrin?" I asked as we moved inside.

He swallowed hard. "If I'd known you were the —" He coughed loudly. "You kept an important piece of information from me, Elspeth Odhweine."

"Ambassador Elmarrin," La'luin called out, her voice echoing in the entryway, "I believe you have other duties to attend to."

The Fae narrowed his eyes and nodded. "Yes… I do."

We continued walking, leaving the pompous ambassador behind.

"Thank you," I said to La'luin.

She smiled and lowered her head in a graceful nod. "This is the eastern wing of Lor As'tuann. You have been granted rooms on the third floor near your friend Raurich."

Grateful that I wouldn't be too far from him, I looked around the palace as we were guided through the tangle of passageways.

The walls were made of polished white stone that glittered with crystal shards, and each brick had been so expertly carved that the joins were barely visible. Tapestries and paintings hung along the length, each depicting a mystical scene full of Fae creatures, battles, and romantic interludes bordering on erotic. Thinking back to the Lor'andann in Un Alari and his penchant for 'tributes', I swallowed hard. The Fae sure were… fluid.

The stairs were made of the same stone, though covered in a thick, earthen-coloured carpet. An elaborate glass dome filled the ceiling and a chandelier made of silver and raw crystal points hung in the centre. Sunlight refracted off the jagged shards, casting flecks of purple over the white walls.

We climbed to the top, passing more cream and gold royal banners, and emerged into another hall like the one downstairs.

La'luin led us to the end and opened a set of double doors, revealing I'd been given the ultimate five-star Fae treatment.

I gave Rory a look and he patted me on the back, following La'luin into the rooms. I had no choice but to join them, my heart fluttering and my head hammering with the word 'agenda'. Were they trying to butter me up? It certainly felt like it.

I ran my fingers over the back of a forest-green and gold brocade couch, staring at the tapestries and garlands of flowers littering every surface. A silver bowl full of alien fruit sat on an elegant table, and Ignis immediately went over to sniff at it.

"Here are your living quarters," La'luin told me. "Through the door to the left, you will find your sleeping quarters and washroom. To the right, are the dining quarters. These rooms have a lovely shaded balcony," she gestured to the floor-to-ceiling windows before us and opened a glass door, "which have a splendid view of the palace grounds and the ocean beyond."

A breeze wafted in and I breathed deeply. It was filled with the tang of salt and the sweet perfume of flowers. Beyond, a thick creeper had twisted around the balustrade, the purple blooms reminding me of wisteria.

La'luin was waiting patiently and I blinked. It took me a moment before I realised she was waiting for my verdict on the rooms.

"They're beautiful," I told her. "Thank you."

"You will be called before the queen when she is ready to receive you," she added. "For now, she bids you rest and recuperate. Food and drink will be brought to you shortly, as well as a selection of clothing. If there is anything else you may desire, all you need do is ask."

The moment La'luin left, Ignis shrank down to his tabby cat shape and circled the room, smelling every piece of furniture at length. He slunk underneath a side table, then leapt up onto an armchair, enjoying his new jungle gym.

I unclipped the buckle on my cloak and threw the heavy fabric over the back of the fancy couch. Sinking down onto the soft cushions, I sighed. Blessed *peace*.

"Do you want me to go?" Rory asked.

"No," I replied. "I haven't seen you in… what, four or five weeks?" I thought for a moment. "If that's how time is measured here. I'm still foggy on that."

"It's an alternate Earth, so time is the same," he told me with a grin. "Time flies here, doesn't it?"

"Yeah."

He sat on the couch beside me and for the first time since we'd met, I didn't know what to say to him. Were my feelings for Altrys messing with my relationship with the Druid? Or was it something else? I didn't have the foggiest.

"La'luin looks like an orange sherbet cone," I declared.

Rory snorted, covering a laugh. "You remind me of a kale smoothie."

My mouth fell open. "*Hey*."

"Too soon?"

"You do realise what all the colours mean, right?"

"Warm colours are Seelie," he replied. "And cool colours—"

"Like green, are Unseelie."

Rory rolled his eyes. "Light, dark, whatever. Maybe I don't understand it, but evil isn't about how someone was born. Evil isn't in someone's DNA. It's about choices."

I didn't want to get into a debate over it. My arse was still sore from three weeks on a saddle and I'd just arrived in another snake pit. Everyone probably had an agenda here and if the Chimera didn't have an agent skulking in the shadows at the Fae court, then I'd drink that kale smoothie.

"This world was nothing like I expected," I said.

"I know what you mean. I was hoping for giant mushroom houses and pointy-eared elves."

"It's a layer cake," I mused. "Or a fancy chocolate with an unknown filling."

"That's either hazelnut praline or cherry liqueur."

"I'd rather the praline. No one likes the liqueur."

Rory frowned. "I have the feeling they've been selective about what they've shown me."

"What do you mean?"

"There's parts of the city they won't speak of or allow me to go. I can't leave the palace without an escort. In fact, I always seem to find myself in the company of La'luin, and it has nothing to do with my natural charm."

I raised my eyebrows. "Natural charm?"

"The queen sees value in the Druids, that's for sure," he went on, ignoring me. "There's politics in play that we have no idea about. Skye was right when she told us that the Fae are tricksters."

"Yeah, I got that feeling."

"You were on your own for weeks," he said. "What was it like?"

"The real world?" I replied. "Well, there's a definite line between Shri'danann and De'ashlide. And another between the Seelie and Unseelie Shri'danann. I wasn't the flavour of the month, even less now since they know who I really am. But when I could disguise myself, the people were nice. The De'ashlide welcomed me in Un Alari."

I looked around my room and into the one next and wasn't sure how to feel about the opulence, while there were people living on top of one another in pieced together houses. Earth had its own class struggles, but it was on full show here—to me, at least. I could only hope that their keeping it from Rory wasn't a sign of anything more sinister.

I sighed and leaned back against the pillows. "I've been here for five minutes and I already want to go back to the forest."

"Spoken like a true Druid," Rory told me.

"How has Ignis been?"

"His usual self," Rory replied. "He hasn't wandered and when he has, La'luin has returned him."

I scowled. "He visits her?"

"I guess." Rory shrugged. "She's not that bad really."

I made a face.

"Fine," he sighed, "she's… uptight and formal."

He could say that again.

"What's with that Altrys guy? All the *shr'lei* I've seen have been Shri'danann, but he's not."

"He's half," I told him. "Like me."

"I see."

"He helped me when I fell through the portal," I went on. "He saved me from a group of thugs who hated Unseelie. And he took two arrows in the shoulder when the Chimera attacked us on the road."

Rory didn't reply at first. Whether he was

uncomfortable about Altrys or regretful he hadn't been there, I didn't know.

"I want to hear all about your adventures," he said after a moment. "Leave nothing out."

I grimaced. Maybe I'd leave a few things out, just for the sake of his heart… and mine.

"And I want to hear all about what you and Ignis have been doing. All of it." I played with my braid, studying the emerald strands. "The queen will summon me soon enough and I have a feeling I'm going to need all the help I can get."

Rory sighed. "Her reputation proceeds her."

My power stirred, letting me know it was still there. "That's what I'm worried about."

2

———

I slept well the first night in Sil Astrad, despite Rory's story playing on my mind.

It filled my dreams with vivid images from his arrival through the portal, to Elmarrin's pompous flailing, to his arrival in the capital… which had caused a stir despite my absence.

He'd told the queen everything, hoping transparency was the best option in asking for her help to rouse a search party. He'd fretted over angering me, but I would have done the same thing in his place. Truth was always the best policy. Well, some of the time, I supposed.

Of course, it hadn't taken long for things in Un Alari to reach a boiling point, so they'd found my location fairly quickly, and in the weeks it had taken me to travel, he'd forged a place for himself amongst the Fae.

It was full steam ahead with his ambassadorial duties, learning how the Fae and the Druids could forge a fruitful alliance. He'd seemed to have made some headway, thanks to La'luin.

And they were quite bewildered by Ignis and his ability to change forms and appear in the most unlikely places. The cat lapped up the attention, as I knew he would.

So far, the queen had welcomed the Darkland Druids into her court and had extended all manner of courtesy. It was what we'd hoped for… but she hadn't met me yet.

I'd been awake for five minutes when a De'ashlide girl scurried in and set up breakfast in the dining room. She kept her gaze down, not daring to lock eyes with me, and said nothing at all before she bowed deeply before hurrying away again.

Were they afraid of me? I couldn't blame them, considering the stories that must be circulating, but it still hurt.

Ignis was absent. He'd stayed with me and Rory until midnight, then slept with me all night, though it seemed his curiosity had gotten the better of him. Lor As'tuann was more exciting—and much larger—than the Warren. I missed that cat, but I couldn't deny him some fun.

I found a green blouse and some simple trousers in the mass of fabric in the closet, and then sat down to eat.

A knock at the door startled me out of my reverie and before I could call out, La'luin strode in.

"Good morning, Elspeth," she said brightly. She was perfectly put together in a simple cream and orange gown, her hair twisted into braids so smooth, they shone.

I felt like a tattered mouse in comparison. The pastry I was eating hovered halfway between the plate and my mouth, and I was sure there were crumbs all over my chin. My hair was a mess and my feet were bare.

However, La'luin didn't seem to notice.

"Where is Ignis?" she asked, looking around the room. "He is such a delightful creature."

"He went out early this morning," I said, putting the pastry down and wiping my chin. "Off exploring, most likely."

"That's a shame. I do like him. Druid magic is unlike anything we've ever seen," she told me. "It's beautiful and complex. His constructed body is a *marvel*."

"You seem awfully interested in him," I said, eyeing her. "Why?"

"Oh, studying magic is my interest, you see. The Shri'danann take it for granted without much thought as to where it comes from or how it works… only that it *does*."

I blinked, startled to find I was warming *a little* to Miss Orange Sherbet. La'luin was the Fae equivalent of a scientist.

"My grandmother made his body," I explained. "It's her... *interest.*"

"Perhaps you might grant me some time to ask you about it? Magic that houses a soul is... Well, it's wonderful!"

I raised my eyebrows. "Perhaps."

"The queen has summoned you," she went on. "If you are ready, I will guide you."

My heart leapt and I smoothed my hands down over my blouse. "You should have led with that."

The Fae smiled and looked me over. "Oh, that won't do at all." She grabbed my hand and pulled me into the bedroom.

Startled, I allowed her to rifle through the closet and hold up dresses against me. "I really don't think—"

"Hush," she interrupted, holding up a simple, mint and cream gown.

"I'm not—"

"This one," she declared. "The queen favours simplicity. She will approve, I am sure. The colour matches your hair."

"What's wrong with what I'm wearing?" I argued. "It's nice, isn't it?"

La'luin glowered at my blouse and trousers. "No."

"But—"

"Impressions matter at court, Elspeth. It is my duty to assist you. You do want to make a good impression for the queen, don't you?"

I sighed. It was clear that no amount of arguing

was going to deter La'luin and her desire to dress me up like a doll.

"*Yes,*" I moaned, my shoulders sinking.

<hr>

Twenty minutes later, we were walking through the palace on our way to see Queen Niarisshia. It wasn't how I'd expected things to go. I thought I'd have some time to prepare, but it seemed she didn't want the *Liash li Ashli* to wander around too long before addressing my presence.

The dress La'luin forced me into wasn't that bad. It laced up the back, had a high neckline, long sleeves, a simple waistline, and the skirt was only one layer of fabric. I didn't know what they spun into the material, but it shimmered like it contained crystal dust, despite feeling like fine linen.

At least I was able to swat away the frilly shoes she'd offered me and could wear my boots. No one would see them hidden under the dress. It was a compromise we could settle on without argument.

La'luin led me through the palace, deep into the heart of the complex, regaling me with stories I barely registered. What was I going to say? Would the queen welcome me, or would she be angry? Would she be grateful for what I did in Un Alari? Maybe a dungeon awaited me at the end of this meeting, or a magical collar—that actually worked this time—to block my powers.

Finally, we stepped through enormous glass doors that led to a vast walled garden. I was taken aback by the scale, and my fears seemed to calm in the presence of so much nature.

La'luin gestured towards the greenery. "The queen awaits your arrival within."

"Here?" I asked.

She nodded once. "Here."

"Okay. then." I hesitated, then turned back. "*A'ladrei.*"

The Fae smiled brightly. "You are most welcome."

Swallowing my nerves, I walked down the path, my boots tapping against the terracotta stones.

There was a wild kind of organised chaos to the garden that sent shivers down my spine. Flowers bloomed in a rainbow of colour, trees stretched towards the blue sky, willows wept over a pond full of fish similar to koi, and the walls of the palace seemed to disappear the deeper I ventured.

It was beautiful… like I'd stepped into another world. The illusion was perfect, but it was just that. An illusion.

I turned a corner and spotted a woman sitting on a bench. Her figure was concealed by a creeping vine laden with the same purple flowers that covered the balcony in my rooms, but I knew who it was.

My first glimpse of the Queen of the Fae wasn't exactly what I was expecting. I'd imagined a fierce woman dressed in finery like I'd seen the Lor'andann and his wife wearing in Un Alari. Her clothes *were* pretty—a simple dress made out of silver and white fabric—but she wore no crown or insignia. There wasn't even an inch of armour plating to be seen.

Her hair was so white it seemed translucent and as she moved, it shone just like starlight. Pale blue eyes met my startled gaze and she smiled.

"Elspeth Odhweine," the queen said, opening her arms in greeting. "I am Niarisshia, Queen of the United Fae. Welcome to Sil Astrad." She patted the bench beside her with long, elegant fingers. "Please, join me."

I sat, folding my hands awkwardly in my lap. She skin reminded me of the inside of a seashell.

"Do you like my garden?" she asked.

"It's beautiful," I replied. "I've never seen anything like it."

"I understand the Druids are creatures tied to nature, much like the Fae."

I nodded. "They are."

Niarisshia said nothing, content to just… be.

I squirmed, uncomfortable with the long silence. Power radiated off her like she was the sun, heating my arm as if I was sitting beside a space heater. My Colours vibrated, picking up on her link to the earth around us. The entire garden basked in her glow, feeding off the light she had cast. *What was she?*

"The tidings from Un Alari were grave indeed," the queen murmured. "I am grateful to you and Altrys, *Shr'lei de Delei'an*. Fate was somewhat cruel to take you from our portal and leave you in the Silver Mountains."

"In hindsight, I'm glad it did."

Her lips thinned and she regarded me with her ethereal eyes. Did she disapprove?

"I have heard Altrys's report," she told me. "A Chimera plot led by the wife of the Lor'andann. *Larel.*"

"I only wanted to help," I said.

"In order to earn my favour."

My cheeks heated and I looked away.

"I know of the Chimera's meddling on Earth," she continued. "The Druid Raurich has told me much of their troubles and regaled me with tales of your assistance in the matter."

"Then you—"

"Know me, Elspeth, *Liash li Ashli.*" She rose, her voice cooling as she locked gazes with me. "I am descended from the oldest race of Fae to ever walk our lands, the Tuatha de Danann. I am descended from their union with the beings known as the Celestines—creatures of starlight-made flesh. The spirit of nature flows through my veins, but also the spirit of war. I have a vision for this realm, as my mother before me, and her mother before her. *I am Queen.*"

And not to be trifled with. Her warning was clear. Niarisshia was not my friend. She was not my equal. And she would do anything to protect her people from the likes of me.

Her expression softened. "To fight for us, you must know who you pledge yourself to."

I rose to her challenge. "And who is that?"

"I am one of the last of my kind, Elspeth, just as you are the only of your kind. A hybrid."

I blinked. "The…Tuatha de Danann and the Celestines are no more?"

"Their demise is a sad story. I am a last remnant of that time. A failed union between our people in hopes of brokering peace."

"They were at war?" I asked.

Niarisshia nodded. "The Tuatha were much like the Chimera in their beliefs. They were extreme and desired power. They travelled through the fabric of space and time, searching for new worlds to claim. Soon they settled on a world much like this one, but with little magic."

"The Earth I came from?" I wondered aloud.

She shook her head. "A different Earth, much the same as yours, but different, nonetheless. Our hand in the fate of your Earth came much later."

The unpredictable nature of her being drove me to silence and I waited for her to continue.

"The human population had no chance against the Tuatha," she went on. "At first, they fought back, despite the odds. However, it did not take long for them to realise they would lose terribly. They had no magic of their own to face the Fae. Submission was the best course of action to save their children from certain death."

"But submitting—"

"Led to slavery." Niarisshia turned to the garden. "The Celestines stepped in when they could take the suffering of the Earth no more. Until then, they had remained in the shadows, unwilling to stand against the Tuatha." They were pacifists, like the Druids. "The Tuatha had scarred what was sacred to them, and it was enough to compel the peaceful race to war… and it drove them to ruin."

I followed her gaze, watching the white tulips sway back and forth. "So they decided to try to make peace?"

"Yes. They both faced extinction, so an alliance was proposed. But one Celestine betrayed them all. *Aoife.* We do not utter her name and I will not speak it again."

I didn't dare ask what the Celestine had done. I waited, hoping Niarisshia would reveal the end of the story.

"There was one child," she added, "spirited away in secret, and it is from him that the royal line is descended. This world was rebuilt from the ashes and a new age of prosperity dawned. The Celestines and the Tuatha live on through me, and I can only hope to keep the peace my ancestors were unable to."

And who was Niarisshia now? It was unclear who was good and who was evil in her tale. Perhaps she was like me, with a light and dark side, merely hoping she made the right choice despite history and fate.

"You're right," I told her. "It is a sad story."

She turned her gaze onto me. "And not an uncommon one."

"The Chimera," I whispered.

"Are an unwelcome reminder of our distant past. They also want the same power the Tuatha lusted after—to remake our world and those like yours in their image."

And one had to go before the world, descended into the same chaos that drove Niarisshia's ancestors to extinction. Hopefully it would be the Chimera, but the jury was still out on that one.

"Do not mistake my story, Elspeth," she added. "The union that bore me, is not the same as the one that bore you."

"I wouldn't dare compare the two. I was born a pawn, nothing more."

"Why are you here, Elspeth?" she asked.

She'd waited all this time to ask.

"I don't know who I am," I replied.

"Oh, I think you know that already." She turned her strange gaze onto me. "People know who they are, though they rarely understand how to put it into words. It is too often confused with what their life stands for. A queen is what I am. I could argue that it is *who* I am, but it is more *what*." Her eyes sparkled.

I've had the same conversation with Altrys when he learned the truth about my powers. People were hung up on what I was without seeing the who. Niarisshia was simply asking me the same question I asked of him but with one caveat—I had to show her.

Fair enough.

"I think I proved myself in Un Alari," I told her. "I could have helped the Chimera and stopped Altrys, but I didn't. I could also be standing with them now, yet here I am in Sil Astrad." Niarisshia's expression remained passive. "I never knew my mother, or that I was Fae or Druid. I grew up human. Thanks to Rory, I was able to connect with my father's family. I know what I am now, and I am death because of it. I'm here to find my family and stop the Chimera."

"Why?"

"Why?" I scoffed. "Death isn't the end, but no one has the right to force anyone to take the next step—not even me. Nature is her own master. The Chimera have no right to it. *I have no right.*"

Niarisshia smiled, her hair fluttering in the breeze. The light made her tresses shine like each strand was made of a billion grains of diamond dust, and for a moment, I was transfixed, forgetting what I was so upset about.

It was then I saw the truth of what Skye had told me about Niarisshia. Young, ambitious, and ruthless. She knew exactly what she was doing and every word she spoke was carefully chosen, even if I didn't understand why.

"Your mother's name was Aurae de Leiran," she said. "If she is dead or alive, I do not know."

I froze, my heart beating erratically. *My mother's name…*

"I will warn you now, Elspeth Odhweine, they

were not a family to be trifled with. Their Shri'danann power was dark and their Unseelie blood ran thick. I cannot speak for your mother or the truth of her story with your Druid father."

I took a deep breath, hoping I wasn't shaking a hornet's nest. "What can you tell me?"

"There is little to tell about the de Leiran family that is not… unsavoury. Their line was famous for their brutality and obsession with forbidden magic. The few times I met your mother, she seemed different, but that was the opinion of a child and I barely remember her. My mother, Queen Aibell, suffered their presence at court to keep the peace, despite the rumours they had aligned themselves with the Chimera. The war that united the Seelie and Unseelie cost us greatly, not only in wealth but diplomacy."

"Could they do things like me?" I asked. "Could they…"

Niarisshia frowned. "It was a rare ability that surfaced in the women in their line. They could control the veil between life and death at will, forcing judgement upon any soul of their choosing. Their blood forced them to darkness and none were safe." *Ominous.*

"They *were*… So my mother was the last de Leiran?"

She inclined her head. "Until you arrived."

"What happened to them?"

"A family like the de Leiran's have many enemies

and with your ability missing several generations, they were besieged." *And killed off one by one.* "Soon, they were few, then none at all." Pending the fate of my mother, of course.

"So, my mother wasn't like me?"

"That I do not know."

There were still more questions that didn't have answers, but now I knew her name. Aurae de Leiran. It was *something.*

"Thank you," I murmured. "You've told me more about my mother in five minutes than I've known in my entire life. Perhaps… Perhaps I can make some peace with it."

Niarisshia nodded sombrely. "I wish it were a happier tale. Your Fae heritage is dark, Elspeth. Perhaps the darkest of them all. Be wary. There are those who still remember." Not to mention a prophecy of destruction that dogged my every step.

It was the story of my supernatural life.

"What now?" I asked. "There is a lot of work to be done. What would you have me do?"

Niarisshia smiled, my words pleasing her. "I know you are eager to fight, but until we know more, venturing out into the world is a danger we must avoid. You are invited to stay here at Lor As'tuann as my guest," she said. "The Chimera have a habit of revealing themselves sooner or later, and I would rather they play their hand first… in a place where I have control."

I rose and nodded, unsure of the protocol. Did I need to bow? Kiss her ring?

"Learn what you can about my people, Elspeth," she added as if she could read my thoughts. "You are one of us. Perhaps your time will be best spent understanding what it is you've pledged to save."

"*A'ladrei,* Queen Niarisshia."

3

———

L a'luin was waiting for me when I left the garden.

"Were you waiting all that time?" I asked, glancing over my shoulder to where Queen Niarisshia still lingered amongst the greenery.

"I thought you might like to see more of Lor As'tuann," she replied. "The library is a marvel. There are over fifty thousand books and scrolls, and even more in the archives."

I did like books, but I knew I wouldn't be able to read any of them. There were few words I knew in the Fae language, and deciphering the letters in their flowing script was near impossible.

"I'd really like to see the *Shr'lei de Delei'an* citadel," I said. "Can you take me there?"

"Why would you want to go there?"

"The queen told me I should learn about the people."

Her eyes narrowed. "You want to see Altrys."

"Of course, I do. Why wouldn't I?"

The Fae sighed. "Very well. This way."

The citadel was linked to Lor As'tuann via a series of armoured gates in the eastern wall. As La'luin guided me, I noticed the beauty of the palace was absent here, and in its place was bleak military standardised colours of bare stone and insignia.

We passed a large hall stuffed full with large tables, a room full of maps and books, and then outside.

The training yard was an open area with a hard dirt surface. At one end was an archery station with targets pinned to bales of hay. At the other, was an area for drills—weapons, hand-to-hand, and large format exercises. This is where we spotted Altrys.

He turned and pivoted, arcing a wooden practice sword through the air. His shirt was rolled up at the sleeves, revealing his toned arm muscles, and it was open at the collar, exposing much more. Where Rory was boyishly handsome, Altrys was very much a man.

I glanced at La'luin and caught her swooning. A flare of jealousy burned in the pit of my stomach and I rubbed my palm over my churning gut.

"You don't have to wait around," I told her. "I've got it from here."

"But you won't get back into the palace without me."

I narrowed my eyes. "I'm sure I can handle it."

"Elsp—"

"They'll let me through if I'm escorted by a *shr'lei*."

La'luin scowled and gave me a tight bow. "Very well."

I snorted as she scurried away, glad to be on my own for a blessed moment. No doubt my movements were being reported, but they wouldn't find anything amiss about me wanting to see Altrys.

Watching him for a moment, I drew in a lengthy breath. Should I kiss him? I didn't know how to handle myself on Earth, let alone know what was appropriate for Fae. Maybe the *Shr'lei de Delei'an* didn't condone public displays of affection. It probably messed with their warrior street cred.

Finally, I walked towards him. "Hey."

Looking up, he eyed me with amusement.

"Nice dress," he said. "I almost didn't recognise you."

"You're hilarious."

"Let me guess. The *Li'deshri* made you wear it."

I nodded and lifted my skirt so he could see my boots underneath.

"Of course. I could never see you wearing those pointy shoes the women at court fuss over." Altrys laughed and set down the practice sword.

"Anyway, what are you doing? Shouldn't you be resting your shoulder?"

He pulled down the neck of his shirt to reveal two red, puckered holes.

My eyes widened. "But—"

"The healers here are skilled," he assured me. "Though I will have to work to regain strength. The muscle was damaged."

"Druids can heal, but I don't think they can fix something like that," I mused. "I've seen them fix a broken nose, cuts and bruises…" Though in my world, it would be bullets, not arrows.

"Speaking of…" Altrys looked over my shoulder. "Where is the Druid?"

I shrugged. "I didn't see him this morning. La'luin dragged me off before I could catch my breath."

"Giving you the grand tour of Lor As'tuann?"

"I saw the queen."

He paused, his gaze casting downward. "And?"

"And I'm standing here, so it wasn't all that bad. She didn't waste any time. I've hardly caught my breath."

"It's been less than a day."

"Is that unusual?"

He nodded. "She likes to make petitioners wait, but you are…"

I scowled and scuffed my toe in the dirt. "You still can't say it?"

"No, it's just…" He looked around the training yard. "The citadel is a safe place, but there are ears, Elspeth."

My cheeks reddened. "Oh, I…"

"Don't worry, I understand." He moved closer. "What did she say?"

I lifted my gaze, not knowing how much to say.

Altrys and I had this *thing* going on between us, but in the grand scheme, we hardly knew one another.

"A lot of things," I began. "About her heritage, about what happened in Un Alari… Well, I'm not exactly sure she's pleased about that. It was hard to tell. She thought I was trying to butter her up."

Altrys frowned. "Butter?"

"To get in her good graces," I replied.

"You were."

"But it wasn't malicious."

"Fae dislike lying, Niarisshia most of all."

"I know that," I grumbled.

"I don't doubt everything she told you is the truth, but she will twist it to work in her favour. Be careful."

"Don't worry, I already got that feeling. Ever since I found out what I am, I've felt that feeling."

Altrys placed his hand on my arm and drew me closer. "You don't have to feel it with me, Elspeth. I know they are just words, but I mean them. What happened to us in Un Alari… it opened my eyes. Niarisshia will see it, too."

I tensed, the truth of my Fae heritage playing on my mind. They were an Unseelie family prone to evil and a slave to the most dangerous power to manifest in their lineage—the black sun. I'd rejected the notion that I was predisposed to darkness weeks ago, but what if I was wrong?

"What is it?" Altrys asked, sensing my hesitation.

"My mother was a de Leiran," I told him. "I know they were bad people, but…"

He paused for a moment. "What did she tell you about them?"

"She said they were into forbidden magic."

Altrys snorted. "That's one way of saying it."

"Like what? Summoning wraiths like that tantankai?"

"Summoning dark creatures, necromancy, coercion, torture… If there was ever a family to align themselves with the Chimera, it was the de Leirans."

I shivered and my Colour flared, the Druidic power responding to my uneasiness. It didn't like being in this world where my control of the veil overpowered it.

"Elspeth, you are nothing like them," he told me. "Don't let anyone tell you otherwise."

"I think my father had something to do with that," I told him. "He raised me away from all this. I didn't know who I was until I'd grown up, and I found the Druids first. It's not the first time his blood guided me away from my Fae powers."

"Then you are more Odhweine than de Leiran."

I sighed. "I'm not sure knowing has made me feel any better."

"It's changed nothing," he said. "You are still the same person you always were, and we face the same dangers we always have."

"The war. Do you think we really stopped it?"

"Adrielle's visions are subjective," Altrys mused. "It's possible we only delayed it, but I seriously doubt the Chimera even have an army. We've seen no evidence to suggest they have any significant numbers to launch a siege against the capital, but they are well-versed in the art of illusion."

"Well, now they know I'm here and working with the Crown, they just might have cause to raise one or reveal their hand." *Just like Niarisshia had planned.*

"If an army marches on Sil Astrad, the queen is the only one who can protect it," he said. "Our army can only do so much."

"How? Like a secret weapon only she can operate?"

Altrys smirked. "Something like that."

"Wait, if she's the last of the Tuatha and the Celestines, then…" I screwed up my face as I realised what it meant.

"The royal line is interbred, and she's not the last. Not yet, anyway."

"This world is more like a fantasy novel than I realised." I sighed. "Well, it won't come to a siege on the capital because I plan to take the fight to the Chimera."

"And how do you propose we do that? No one knows where the Chimera congregate. The location of their stronghold has been one of their greatest mysteries."

"I know. To find them, I'll need the help of the people who have the resources, which means I need to show Niarisshia that she can trust me despite the prophecy. Her agenda is her own business, my concern is stopping the Chimera once and for all."

"Those are dangerous words, Elspeth," Altrys warned. "Niarisshia's agenda may not be one you like."

"I know, but it might just be a risk I have to take to see this done."

He lowered his gaze and took my hand in his. Warmth spread through my body and I wished we could just *be* for a moment, but there were too many variables hanging over our heads.

The Chimera were more of an enigma now than ever. No one knew where they came from or where they hid, or even how many there were. We'd been flying blind back on Earth, but I'd thought the Fae would have known more.

"Altrys?"

He paused.

"What kind of Fae are the Chimera? They cover themselves in illusions to look human, but their true faces…"

"Does it matter?"

"I guess not. I just never thought about it before."

"They *are* Fae, just like you and I, Elspeth. It's just that their bodies are ravaged through the rituals and sacraments of their religion."

I shivered. "They twist their bodies willingly?"

Altrys nodded. "Faith is powerful. Maybe even more powerful than magic itself."

"*Faith,*" I whispered. I was going to need a lot of my own in the coming days, weeks, months… maybe even years.

How long was this going to drag out for? There was no way of telling, which was frustrating to say the least, but I could do one thing to ease my mind.

"Altrys?"

"You ask a lot of questions."

"I know, but it's important."

He smiled and rubbed his thumb over the back of my hand. "What would you ask of me, Elspeth Odhweine?"

"There's going to be a lot of fighting in my near future," I said. "Would you help me train?"

"Are you sure you need it? I saw how you fought in the forest."

"That was with the help of magic," I argued. "I don't want to rely on it."

He stared at me, surprise etched in his handsome features. "You are a strange creature, Elspeth. Strange and wise."

"I take it I'm not your typical Shri'danann."

"I worked that out a month ago."

I raised my eyebrows. "So?"

"I will train with you," he replied. "Around my other duties."

I clapped my hands and fist-pumped the air. "Yes!"

The *Shr'lei* shook his head, the unfamiliar gesture yet another thing that perplexed him about me.

"Altrys? Just one more thing."

He chuckled and picked up his practice sword.

"Ask me anything. I've become used to your interrogations."

"I couldn't help but notice… When La'luin brought me into the citadel, I saw no De'ashlide."

Altrys sighed. "The *Shr'lei de Delei'an* is exclusively Shri'danann."

"Is that why you were in Un Alari?" I asked. "To get away from the capital?"

"There are… expectations here," he replied. "One's I don't like."

I got it. As part De'ashlide, to keep his place amongst the *Shr'lei de Delei'an*, he had to compensate for his weakened magic in other places. I didn't blame him for taking the remote assignment. Prejudice was as rampant here as it was on Earth.

"Well, let's give them something to actually talk about," I said, taking the sword from his hand. "This will feed the rumour mill for *months*."

Altrys laughed, his expression softening. "Maybe change out of the dress first."

———

I ran into Ignis in the hallway on my way back to Lor As'tuann. He prowled towards me in his tiger form, his tail swishing back and forth.

"Hey, you," I said. "You do like to wander, huh? Find anything good?"

The cat headbutted my leg and nudged me down the corridor towards the stairs.

"Where are we going?"

He didn't reply, of course. Ignis was many things, but vocal wasn't one of them. Sometimes I found myself wanting to hear him speak, but his soul was too patchy to allow much of anything from his former life to remain. He'd shown me the few fleeting images he did recall—a ruined castle, a tall man with a sword, and the sacrifice he'd made to save the people he'd left behind—but it wasn't much to go on.

I followed the tiger through the maze of Lor As'tuann until he stopped outside a door near where my own rooms sat. He'd led me to Rory.

Rapping my knuckles on the door, I eased it open and stepped into the room.

Rory was engrossed in an open book as he paced up and down the length of the room, passing by a massive open fireplace that crackled with a small blaze despite the warmth outside. Strangely enough, woodsmoke carried the scent of home.

He'd also cleared out a space where various couches and ornamental plants had once sat. They were shoved up against the far wall, and in their place, he'd assembled a miniature workshop like the one he'd built back in the Warren. Crystal shards littered the table, along with papers full of notes and drawings. The ornate rug was rolled back, revealing the stone floor underneath. I recognised the runes drawn on the speckled marble and frowned.

He was messing around with portals again.

When he saw me, his eyebrows rose. "Nice dress."

"I hope you're joking because I hate this thing."

Rory shook his head and gestured for me to come in. I stood beside him, looking over the notes on the table as Ignis looked for a comfy spot to sleep. The tiger had seen this all before.

"What are you working on?" I asked.

"While you've been horseback riding all over the countryside, La'luin has been helping me understand portals," he said. "They don't know much, but every piece helps."

I raised my eyebrows. "Are you sure it's wise mucking around with that stuff in your bedroom?"

"It was one of the reasons we came here. Anyway, I haven't opened any portals. I'm studying their composition."

"What about the Fae portals? Are they the same as ours?"

"They're slightly different, but essentially the same."

"That makes no sense."

"La'luin believes they were created by the Tuatha de Danann," he explained. "They invaded an alternate Earth thousands of years ago, but she thinks they could have begun preparations to cross into our world, too. There are portals all over Ireland, and they extend into England, Wales, and Scotland."

"Skye said the Crescent Witches locked them all a thousand years ago," I mused. "And they only reopened the one." I wondered if they knew there were more. It seemed unlikely.

"Maybe that's how the Chimera got to Edinburgh," Rory went on. "They found a dormant portal and were somehow able to open it."

"Or they were stuck there for a thousand years. Owen said as much."

"How can they live for a thousand years?"

"How can Druids?" I asked. "Altrys said the Chimera twist their bodies through magic and ritual like a religious sacrifice. Maybe they do it because it extends their lives? Maybe that's how they survived on Earth when so many others didn't." Rory's eyes narrowed at the mention of the *shr'lei*, but I chose to ignore it. "Do you think La'luin can help you find the Darklands?"

Rory shrugged. "I want to trust them, but we've been through too much for me to blindly follow her lead."

I grunted and glanced at Ignis, who'd decided to go to sleep on the couch… upside down.

"What's that look for?" Rory asked.

"She's rather interested in Ignis," I replied. "Should I be worried?"

"La'luin is okay."

"She's the queen's personal assistant," I said, picking up a crystal. "There's a massive conflict of interest."

"Yes, which is why I haven't told her everything. They don't know about the homeland and I'd rather keep it that way."

I nodded. "Seems reasonable."

"Anyway, what have you been doing today? Your dress is filthy."

"I've been training with Altrys," I told him. "Which is something you ought to give thought to."

He made a face. "I can fight."

"You can, but they're better. These aren't the same Chimera we fought on Earth, Rory. When they came after us on the road…"

His scowl deepened. "I can fight."

"Have you seen the *Shr'lei de Delei'an* citadel?" I asked. "There are rooms full of fancy armour and weapons. It's incredible. If there's a weapon or skill you want to learn, I'm sure they know it."

"*Elspeth*," he snapped.

I tensed. "What?"

"I don't want to hear about that guy or his bloody sword."

"*O mo chreach*," I said in Gaelic. "You're jealous? Rory, *don't*."

"I can't help it," he cried, turning his back on me. "You keep pushing me towards Vanora, and I don't want to hurt her, but that's duty, not love."

"Rory, we've been through this."

He sighed. "And nothing's changed."

"I've been back a day."

"And you've proved that you don't need me."

I grabbed his arm, my Colour rippling as it wrapped around his, and forced him to look at me. "I need you. We need each other."

His brow furrowed.

"Rory, I spoke to Niarisshia this morning."

"You should have led with that."

I took his hands in mine. I didn't touch people without meaning it, so he would understand that I was serious.

"I need to tell you everything," I murmured. "I think… I think things are going to change around here and not for the better."

"What do you mean? What did she tell you?"

I reached for my Colour and began to weave a delicate prism. Rory raised his eyebrows but joined his power with mine, helping me cast a bubble of privacy around us.

Then, I told him everything.

4

For the first time in months, my life began to settle into a routine.

Breakfast and dinner were spent with Rory, strategising and theorising everything from the Chimera to portals. Then during the day, I ventured out into the palace as far as I was able.

I wasn't invited to court, all my meals were brought to my rooms, and the palace staff seemed happy to avoid me at all costs. It was probably for the best, considering I was a de Leiran. I still wasn't sure how to feel about it and solitude was where I found strength.

However, La'luin was my constant shadow. Every time I wanted to leave my rooms, she would escort me, using the opportunity to teach me about the history of the Fae. We both knew she was a spy dressed up as a glorified babysitter, but she was desperate to study Ignis's construct. It gave me some leeway to bend a few rules, and training with Altrys was one of them. Ignis began joining us in the citadel, though all he did was sit around as Altrys and I worked on strengthening both his healing shoulder and my skills.

Lor As'tuann was a beautiful place, but it was cold. Life swelled around me, yet I couldn't reach out and touch it—save for the few people who knew me well enough to want to.

"You look different," Rory told me one morning, almost a week after I'd arrived in the capital.

We were having breakfast in my rooms, which consisted of a platter of fruit, pastries, juice, a coffee-like hot drink, and the Fae equivalent of a full English breakfast—eggs, bacon, tomato, sausage, and beans. Whatever their proper name was, I had no idea. Rory avoided the meat, but I tried everything.

"How?" I asked, wrinkling my nose at the taste of the bacon. It was so not the same. I offered it to Ignis, who sniffed at it, then turned up his nose.

"You were so quiet," he replied, "and having existential crises every two minutes. You were exhausting."

"I had every right to freak out. You came across like a total nut job."

He chuckled and turned back to his notebook.

I stared at him for a moment, remembering the night we'd first met. He'd been trying to save me from the Chimera, but I thought he was attacking me. I'd tried to punch him in the face, but my fist never connected. Now, after all the battles I'd fought, there was no way I would miss.

My wistful smile faded, and I shoved a forkful of beans into my mouth before Rory caught me staring.

After I'd met the queen, my first thought had been for Altrys, not Rory. After all we'd been through, I should have gone to see Rory the moment I'd finished talking with Niarisshia.

Even when I'd gone off on my own, he'd always been there. It was Rory and me against the Chimera. It was Rory and me fighting side by side. It was Rory and me travelling through the portal.

Now Altrys was part of the equation.

Sighing, I was beginning to understand why romantic relationships were so complicated. Maybe I hadn't been missing out on much after all.

"What's that for?" Rory asked, looking up.

"Nothing," I murmured, looking out the window.

Outside, I could see one of the towers along the wall of the palace. It glittered pink and orange in the sunrise, looking more like crystal than the starlight of its namesake city.

"La'luin wants to hang out with you today," Rory said.

"Huh? Why?" I scowled. "She 'hangs out' with me every day."

"She wants to show you her workshop and look at Ignis's construct."

I shook my head. "I've got trust issues."

"I think you should let her," he told me. "She

can't do anything to manipulate our Colour. Our abilities are completely separate to the Fae's. Besides, her abilities might help you with your own."

My defences came up and I eyed him warily. "Her abilities?"

"La'luin is Seelie, but her magic is similar to yours. She… Ah, maybe she ought to explain it herself."

"Have you seen the way they look at me? La'luin is Niarisshia's spy. All she wants is to find something to twist against me. They're looking for an excuse to put me in shackles and control my power."

"Elspeth, they don't know you, that's all," he reassured me. "Give them some time and they'll see."

"I don't like sitting here. It's like waiting for a storm we know is coming and doing nothing to prepare."

"Niarisshia is playing it safe, which is her prerogative, but La'luin is fair. Her position demands her to be authoritative, but her intentions are good. She wants to be your friend, Elspeth."

I folded my arms over my chest. "You seem quite taken with her."

"It's not like that." He leaned forwards, resting his elbows on the table, and gave me a heated look. "You know it's not like that."

"*Rory.*"

"I'm a good judge of character," he went on, sitting back. "I saw your potential when everyone else didn't, so you can trust me on this."

I resisted the urge to pout.

"You're not the only one who the Fae avoid," he added. "I'm an anomaly, too. They're interested in our ability to open portals, just like the Chimera were with your father, but what they don't know is," he grinned and held his hands like he was cupping an invisible ball, "how much we like origami."

I stared at him, my mouth falling open. "You didn't."

"When negotiating an alliance, it's best not to go to the table with all your best cards, especially when the other party has more to gain." He pressed his finger to his lips and nodded towards the door.

La'luin breezed in a moment later, her orange dress bouncing like a powderpuff cloud. She didn't knock, which was becoming her norm. I didn't even want to mention my horror when she'd walked in on me in the nude the day before. The Fae were *definitely not* prudes.

"Good morning, Raurich and Elspeth." She smiled brightly as she spotted her favourite cat sitting beside my chair, waiting for a handout. "And Ignis."

To my astonishment, the cat began to purr. Maybe I was just reacting to her frilliness. I was so not a frilly kind of woman.

"Elspeth, Altrys has duties to attend to today, so he will be unavailable to train with you. I wonder…" She glanced at Ignis. "Would you like to accompany me to my workshop?"

Rory kicked me under the table and gave me a look that said, 'told you so'.

"What duties?" I asked.

"Secret *shr'lei* business," Rory drawled. "*Probably.*"

This time, I returned his kick with a powerful one of my own.

"*Air do shocair,* Elspeth," he cursed in Gaelic.

"Ignis," I called, "do you want to spend time with La'luin today?" I leaned over and met his gaze. "She wants to probe you."

Rory snorted and Ignis let out an amused rumble.

"Your world is peculiar," the Fae mused with a creased brow. "So very peculiar."

The three of us left Rory to his breakfast and wandered through the hallways into a part of the palace I hadn't seen before. Ignis padded beside us, his footsteps silent on the plush carpet.

"How have you been finding Lor As'tuann?" La'luin asked.

"Isolating."

She frowned and inclined her head. "Yes, I suspect it would be. It's not personal, Elspeth. The Fae have long memories and your family—"

"I share their blood by birth, but I never knew them. They're not my family. I'm an Odhweine and before that, I was human—my world's version of a De'ashlide. My father and the Druids are my family."

"Yes…" She squirmed. "I didn't mean…"

"I know," I told her. "You're a product of your environment. That's how life works."

"I would so like to get to know you," she went on. "Altrys spoke highly of you in his report."

I hesitated as we stopped beside a closed door. "You read Altrys's report? What did it say?"

"Nothing that you wouldn't already know, I suspect." She smiled and opened the door. "Come. We've arrived."

La'luin's workshop was nothing like I'd envisioned. It was bright and airy, though every available space was littered with magic devices, crystals, gemstones, vials, herbs, and books.

I did a lap of the room while La'luin beamed proudly. This was her pride and joy. I could see why Rory liked her so much.

Stopping by the large table in the centre of the room, I studied a complex device made up of metal tubes and glass lenses.

"It's a seeing glass," the Fae explained. "You can put things underneath it to see them up close. The glass can be focused."

"Oh, its a microscope." I peered through one of the lenses, but there was nothing on the slide underneath it.

"You have similar things in your world?"

I nodded and looked around at the books on the shelves. Some of them appeared to be her personal journals, and others were written in the scripted Fae language.

"May I?" She gestured to Ignis.

I nodded and continued poking through her

things. When I didn't find anything incriminating, I leaned against the table and watched her prod at Ignis's prisms.

"His construct is… I don't have a word for it," she murmured, running her hand over his coat. "His prisms shimmer like light refracting off crystal."

"Druidic Colour manifests as crystal sometimes," I told her. "Crystal is at the core of a lot of things we do."

"Yes, crystal does seem to be one of the universe's natural building blocks. Mineral, fire, water, and air. Everything is constructed around these basic principles."

I remembered some of the things I'd learned from my dad about the make-up of nature—atoms, molecules, protons, and all of those fancy words I never had a chance to learn about in university. He was an environmental scientist, as well as being a Druid, and had passed a little of his knowledge to me before he'd died.

The universe was more complex than a little fire and water, but it was too much to debate right now. Still, I wondered what the Fae knew of science. Perhaps they didn't need it while they had their magic.

"Has Raurich told you about my abilities?"

I shook my head.

"I am what our people call a Soulweaver," she explained. "It's a spiritual ability that allows me to see into someone's soul."

"To do what?" I asked, watching her carefully.

"To see truth."

I sighed. I wondered if she'd already tried her powers on me. "Now I know why you're the queen's sidekick."

"Sidekick?"

"Her *Li'deshri*."

La'luin smiled. "Yes, though it's not all I can do." She threaded her fingers through Ignis's fur. "I think I may be able to help him."

"Help him, how?" I glanced at Ignis, who didn't seem distressed by this revelation. Perhaps he already knew.

"I cannot repair his broken soul, but I may be able to bring pieces of it back. I sense... There are some things that are foggy within him, while others are gone completely."

"It's up to him." I looked to Ignis. "Is that what you want?"

His tail flicked back and forth, and he nodded, which was a strange thing to see a tiger do.

"Okay," I said to La'luin. "He's good with it, so do your best."

The Fae sat cross-legged before him and placed her hands on his brow. Her eyes fluttered closed and I sensed the hum of her magic as it flowed through her fingers and into Ignis's construct.

The prisms rippled, but he held his shape, his head drooping as La'luin's magic pulsed.

After fifteen minutes or so, I was beginning to

wonder if anything was going to happen. Then I heard my name being called.

'*Elspeth.*'

Started, I looked around. La'luin opened her eyes and sighed, oblivious.

"There you are," the Fae murmured. "Welcome back."

'*Elspeth,*' the voice came again. This time, it was accompanied by a nudge from Ignis.

"Ignis?" I whispered.

I knelt before the tiger and cupped his furry cheek. His whiskers bristled and he tapped my knee with his massive paw.

"That was you," I whispered. "*You have a voice.*" I looked at La'luin, who was beaming. "Can you hear him? He said my name. He said…"

She shook her head. "He seems to be talking to you, and you alone. Cats are selective about who they like, as you must already know."

"How is this possible?"

"He had magic," La'luin told me. "Magic is infused with our souls and passes with us when we shed our mortal bodies."

Of course. He could change his construct, appear and reappear at will, and walk into death with me, but I never knew his voice could return. *I could talk to him.*

I took a deep breath and found his gaze. "Do you remember your name?"

'*I-I—*' He lowered his head. '*Is… Is… I cannot.*'

"So, it began with the letter 'I'," I mused. "That's why you liked Ignis so much. Not to worry, hey?"

He purred and brushed up against me, almost knocking me on my arse. Now he had a voice, he didn't seem to know what to say. His construct had overtaken what humanity his soul retained and now he was more feline than man.

My smile faded as I ran my palm over his black and blue flank.

"Ignis?"

He looked up at me with his big, hazel eyes.

"I asked you before, but I have to know… The Druids made you and you never had a choice. Do you… Do you resent Delilah for catching your soul?"

'No,' he said. *'She saved me from being erased. I have a chance to do more.'*

I felt tears prickle my eyes and I threw my arms around his neck. "Oh, Ignis."

'I will help you,' he purred. *'I was meant to find you.'*

"Me too," I whispered. "Me too."

5

———

Ignis didn't know any more of his story. Like his soul, his magic was shattered… but not broken.

He had a voice, thanks to La'luin, but his memory of his past life was still as hazy as the images he'd shown me in death. He told me he felt connected to the spirit world in much the same way I was, but if that was linked to his own magic or something that happened when Delilah created him, we didn't know.

We walked side by side through the palace, following La'luin. I was so grateful for what she'd done for Ignis, I'd agreed to let her show us the library.

She was prattling on about some obscure branch of Fae history that I was only half listening to when I felt the tingle of Ignis's thoughts penetrate my own.

'Elspeth,' he said. *'Something's wrong.'*

I wasn't in a position to question him. He'd spent the last month wandering Lor As'tuann, so if he sensed something was out of place, then something was out of place.

'Where?' I asked as I cast out my senses.

'Behind us.'

I felt it at the same time Ignis's voice echoed in my mind. A coldness swirled through the palace and it was moving towards us.

Reaching out, I grasped La'luin's arm and pulled her back into an alcove. The curtains rustled as we passed, the heavy fabric settling almost instantaneously.

My skin prickled and my Colour stirred, reacting to the unknown.

"Elspeth, What—"

"*Shh,*" I hissed.

La'luin blinked as if I'd slapped her.

Ignis slunk into the alcove, his prisms fluttering as he considered changing shapes. A moment after he'd moved behind the silver and gold curtains, the air shifted again.

Peering out into the hall, I swallowed a gasp as a thick, white mist billowed into the hall where we'd just been standing. It paused an arm's length from our hiding spot, the essence solidifying in several places. A head, a shoulder, and an arm took shape within and my heart lurched. I had a bad feeling about this.

La'luin grasped my hand as we hid, waiting to see if we'd been discovered. She was afraid, I could feel it in her touch, but I wasn't. I was too busy trying to figure out what it was. There was intelligence within the vapour, hiding just out of reach.

Finally, the mist whipped around, billowing into a thick cloud before thinning out and moving down the hall away from us.

What was that? Was it… a spirit?

"Did you see that?" La'luin whispered, her voice trembling.

I nodded. "Whatever it is, it's not good."

Slipping out from behind the curtains, I looked down the hall. The mist lingered ahead, out of sight, but within the range of my magic.

As if it'd been waiting for me, the creature began to move once more, progressing through the palace at a steady pace. There was only one thing to do when someone like me saw something dodgy. Follow it.

"Where are you going?" La'luin hissed.

"I'm following it."

"I'm not a warrior," she whispered. "I-I don't know what to do. We should call for the guards."

"And scare the thing away?" I shook my head. "I want to know what it's doing here."

"B-but—"

"Stay behind me," I said, nudging her backwards. "And keep quiet. Ignis will protect you."

"What about you?"

I snorted. "I'll be fine."

La'luin nodded and slid her fingers into Ignis's black and blue coat for comfort.

'Careful, Elspeth,' Ignis said. *'It knows you're here.'*

Meaning, it could be a trap. It was just another chapter in a long line of chapters entitled 'let's manipulate the *Liash li Ashli*'. I was used to it by now.

We followed at a distance, only catching glimpses of the white mist as it darted around corners. We climbed a set of stairs and crossed a walkway that stretched across a corner of the queen's gardens, then into a lavish crystalline part of the palace. The walls were made out of cloudy, white quartz and veins of gold sliced through the rock here and there. I'd never seen anything like it.

Ahead, the corridor was dotted with ornate doors. Each was made out of chocolate-coloured wood and inset with crystal eight-pointed stars—*tuathade'shri*—bordered with more pure gold.

The door nearest was slightly ajar and sunlight streamed through the gap, casting a refracted rainbow across the stone floor. Glancing down the hall, I didn't see any guards or servants. We were alone, which wasn't an anomaly in the sprawling building, but this part of the palace was usually bustling. This wing looked important, like—

"Elspeth," La'luin whispered, "these are the queen's quarters."

"What?" My blood ran cold and I swore in Gaelic. "*Stay back.*"

Wasting no time, I burst into the room. My skin turned blue as the veil bled into my fingers and crawled up my arms.

Niarisshia was sprawled out on the floor, the mist

on top of her. A knife glinted in the sunlight streaming through the crystal windows, the edge angled towards her throat.

I moved like lightning.

Striding across the room, I lifted my blackened hand and wrenched the veil around the humanoid mist. I pulled, dragging the creature away from the queen.

The knife clattered to the floor as I held the writhing mist in an invisible grasp. I hadn't even touched it, not that I could have. This world had amplified my power yet again and not a moment too soon.

I growled, my vision blurred, and I slammed the creature against the wall as hard as I could. The quartz cracked and the thing let out a human cry of pain, then swore in Gaelic.

"Enough!" the queen commanded.

Startled, I loosened my grip and the mist slipped through my fingers. It swirled across the room in an angry whirlwind, then collided with a side table against the far wall.

I reached for the discarded knife, not trusting what was going on, but Niarisshia shook her head.

"That won't be necessary," she said.

The mist swirled angrily, then as I blinked, became solid.

A woman sat on the side table, her legs swinging over the edge. She twisted a lock of golden hair around her slender finger and laughed like she'd just witnessed a comedy routine.

I stared open-mouthed, totally confused. She looked exactly like Sage, Skye's daughter… Sage was in Ireland. In another world. Who also had *black* hair.

"I'm Hazel," she said in an Irish accent. "From the look on your face, I assume you've met my sister."

Suddenly, I remembered Skye telling me about her other daughter… who lived with the Fae. "You're—"

"A Witch. A Crescent, to be precise."

"What's going on here?" My brow creased and I looked at Niarisshia, my suspicion and anger beginning to boil. "Someone better explain… *and fast.*"

"I'm just following orders," Hazel said, flexing her fingers around her magic. "I'm just the queen's trophy. *Oops.* I meant, *ward.*"

"That's enough, Hazel," Niarisshia said, rising gracefully. "You performed beautifully."

The Witch sighed and glared at me. "Can I go? She's kind of freaking me out."

Niarisshia nodded and she scurried away, clearly bored with the whole thing. It didn't take a genius to see that Hazel was nothing like her twin sister, even though they were almost identical.

"Words mean little to me, Elspeth Odhweine," the queen said as the door closed behind the Witch. "Words are powerful in the hands of the wrong people. They can be twisted and manipulated until they mean whatever the speaker wants. You told me you wanted what was best for this world. You told me you want to destroy the Chimera before they use you to destroy this world."

"*I do*," I snapped as the black sun retreated. Warmth spread through my limbs, but it didn't nothing to thaw my frosty mood.

Niarisshia stepped towards me, her gaze piercing into mine like razor-sharp icicles. "How can I be sure? Words, Elspeth, are meaningless to me."

My expression began to fall as I realised what had just happened.

"This was a test," I murmured on the brink of relief and chaos all at once. The veil pulsed, brushing against my fingers.

Let me go, it called. *Let me have her. How dare she.*

The queen glanced at my hands and smirked. "And you passed."

I glared at La'luin, who was clutching Ignis's fur so tightly I could see the grimace on the cat's face.

"Were you in on it?" I demanded. "Was our whole day together a manipulation?" I wondered if Altrys was really off doing other *shr'lei* duties or if that was a lie, too.

La'luin shook her head, her eyes brimming with tears. "I-I thought… *My queen*." She stumbled, intending to fall to her knees before Niarisshia, but I caught her. No one was bowing to anyone in this room, no matter how high their standing.

"You must understand, Elspeth," Niarisshia said,

"I am responsible for every life in this world. From the Shri'danann to the De'ashlide. From the animals to the insects. From the flowers to the trees. The elementals no longer concern themselves with the Fae and our troubles. I am the only one who stands against the chaos. There is no room for failure."

I wasn't so sure about the elementals. I'd seen them in the forest when Altrys was wounded. *Ak'ande la. Save him…*

'*Elspeth, she has a point,*' Ignis said.

I shivered, the sound of Ignis talking in my head still unfamiliar. '*It doesn't mean I 'have to like it,* I told him.

At the end of the day, I'd won the trust of the Fae at the cost of my pride, *but…* There was always a but.

"La'luin," the queen said, "would you escort our honoured guest back to her quarters? Her work begins tomorrow."

I narrowed my eyes. "What work?"

"It's time for the world to know the *Liash li Ashli* fights for them, Elspeth Odhweine," she replied. "It will be the ultimate insult to the Chimera… and if your mother is alive, she will no doubt try to contact you."

Niarisshia wanted to dangle me in front of a legion of starved carnivores to see what happened? I was bait…and I didn't have a choice.

What was I saying about 'buts'?

I stewed in my anger as La'luin guided Ignis and I back to my rooms in the east wing. I should have been excited that I could now speak to the tiger, but instead I was livid. Niarisshia had just tricked me into becoming the thing I never wanted to be—a pawn.

Who was I to defy a queen? I controlled death itself, but even I had to bow before Niarisshia. I was Fae, which made me her subject by default.

Rory was waiting for us when we arrived.

"What happened?" he asked. "The whole palace is talking about an attack."

"That didn't take long," I drawled, pushing into my rooms. "The rumour mill is already spreading disinformation. The CIA could learn a thing or a thousand from these people."

"She's upset," La'luin said to the Druid. "I was not a part of the queen's plot, I swear it."

Ignis swept past Rory and his eyes widened. Whatever the tiger had said to the Druid, it must have been good.

"Ignis?" he called, following us inside. "*O mo chreach.*"

La'luin hovered at the door. "I will fetch you on the morrow, Elspeth. I will make sure dinner is served here for the both of you tonight. Ignis, any special requests?"

I wasn't listening to a word she said, instead I kept my ears peeled for the moment she left so I could rant at Rory. He would understand.

"Ignis can talk?" he said as the door closed. "Did

La'luin…" He shivered as Ignis spoke to him, but his voice was silent to me. It seemed the cat hadn't learned how to multi-task yet.

"I just saved the queen from a fake assassination attempt," I raged. "I thought she was about to get stabbed by a Chimera, but no, it was a bloody Witch made out of mist!"

"A Witch?" Rory's eyes widened, his shock at Ignis's voice forgotten.

"It was Hazel," I told him. "Skye and Boone's daughter. Did you know she was here?"

"No, I had no idea." He shook his head. "I told you they've been keeping things from me. There's only so much I can do to get past their magic with Colour. The two aren't that compatible, you know."

"I do know." Which was why it may still work in our favour somewhere down the line. If things kept going the way they were, I had a feeling we might need to stage a breakout. Now that I knew some of the land, I could phase us outside the walls of Sil Astrad.

"The whole thing was staged," I went on. "I can't believe she'd do something like that."

"Niarisshia comes from a long line of inbreeding," Rory told me. "There's a reason the Druids—"

"I get it," I interrupted. "I don't need to hear it again."

"That's beside the point. The royal line has dwindled to three as far as I can tell. Niarisshia, her aunt, and a brother who she's probably going to… *you know.*"

"So, you're saying she's a crazy inbred—"

"*Elspeth.*"

'*I don't like the way she treated you,*' Ignis told me. '*She has an unpredictable… feeling.*'

'*And it's not from inbreeding,*' I replied.

'*The Fae like to trick. Be wary.*'

I snorted. He could say that again. Niarisshia had told me she was the only one of her kind.

"Are you talking to Ignis in your head?" Rory asked. "I've got serious FOMO right now."

'*She's a means to an end,*' Ignis added. '*I think you should see if this plan forces the Chimera to reveal their whereabouts.*'

I raised a brow at Ignis. 'In other words, calm down?'

He purred and nudged his head against my leg.

"What's going on?" Rory demanded. "I'm standing right here."

"We're not talking about you," I replied with an eye roll. "I'm just… pissed is all. I'll calm down." I glanced at Ignis and my anger began to ease. "You can talk. Let's celebrate that because tomorrow's going to be the beginning of something… unknown."

Rory stepped closer. "Tomorrow?"

"Tomorrow…" I shook my head, already tired. "Tomorrow we go into Sil Astrad and declare war… *Queen's orders.*"

6

After dinner, Rory left me and Ignis to continue to work on his portals.

I made him promise to go to bed early, and even though he agreed, I knew my pleas fell on deaf ears. Tomorrow we'd go into Sil Astrad and who knew what would be waiting for us. Definitely not souvenir shopping and opened top tourist busses.

I flopped back onto the couch and sighed. Ignis leapt up beside me, melding his tabby cat shape along my side. His prisms sparkled as the last of his tiger form retreated and he began to purr.

'Have you been into Sil Astrad?' I asked. *'There wasn't much to see on the way in.'* Though I'd made some pretty bleak observations.

'The Fae wouldn't allow Rory and I to leave the palace,' Ignis replied. *'Not until you were found.'*

'And they haven't since…' I mused. *'Until now.'*

'She was testing your loyalties by using the Witch.'

'*I know she had a point, but—*'

'*She's painting you as a hero to take the fear of you out of the people, Elspeth.*'

'*For her own gain,*' I argued hotly. '*I'm just another piece on Niarisshia's chess board.*'

'*Perhaps, but if it gets us closer to the Chimera…*'

'*This is about more than saving the Fae realm,*' I told him. '*It's about my family and stopping my prophecy.*'

'*Yes, but it comes with a world full of collateral.*'

He was so right; I began to believe he'd been a psychologist in his past life. A warrior monk who wielded the blade of the mind.

'*Niarisshia wants to parade me around the city like a trophy,*' I grumbled. '*Like a piece of meat. What if something goes wrong?*'

'*Then we will handle it.*'

I raised my eyebrows. '*We?*'

'*I might be a man living in a cat's body, but I know things.*'

'*I'm sure you do.*'

'*I remember…*' He lowered his head and narrowed his amber eyes. '*A ruined castle. A crystal.*'

'*I remember you had a pretty bad-arse sword,*' I told him.

'*There was someone there at the end. I did something to protect them, but…*' He flexed his claws, the points kneading into the couch cushions. '*The memory is gone.*'

His frustration and longing flowed through our connection and I swallowed back the lump in my throat. I couldn't do anything but stroke his coat, hoping my touch soothed the ache in his broken soul.

I didn't know what I was expecting, but Ignis's

voice was so clear and concise, it was like I was talking to the man, not the construct. It was easy to forget that was exactly who he was. He'd always been a cat to me.

'I'm so happy I can finally talk to you,' I told him.

'Me, too.'

'I'm sorry you can't remember your name, or—'

The cat headbutted me on the nose and I swatted him away.

'I'm glad to be here with you, Elspeth,' he murmured. *'To help you and the Druids has given my new life purpose.'*

'Really?' I scratched behind his ears.

'Altrys approaches.'

I lifted my head as a knock at the door echoed through the room. *'How did you know?'*

'I told you, I know things. I'll bet you fifty quid.'

My mouth fell open. *'What does a cat need fifty quid for?'*

'Online shopping.'

"Elspeth?" Altrys called.

"Yes," I replied, glaring at Ignis. "I'm here! Come in!"

Sitting up as Altrys came in, Ignis leapt onto the floor and stalked around the *Shr'lei.* The Fae promptly stared at Ignis in much the same way Rory had.

"La'luin helped him get his voice back," I explained, righting myself. "The first thing he did was try to hustle me."

"Hustle?"

"Swindle me out of all my money," I explained and eyed the cat. "Which is worthless in this world."

Altrys smirked as Ignis flicked his tail and slid through the crack into the hall. The cat was off for the evening, likely seeking out Rory so he could annoy him.

"You can't fault him for taking advantage of his newfound freedom," the *Shr'lei* told me as he closed the door. "A voice is important."

"I know. I'm glad I can finally talk to him. He's quite insightful."

Altrys nodded and sat beside me, his presence calming. He wore a soft tan shirt and black trousers, and I noticed he'd shaved. Shame, I liked the stubble.

"I heard about what happened with the queen," he began. "You seem…"

"I've calmed down. You should have seen me earlier."

"What happened?"

I told him about the mist and bursting into the queen's rooms to find her on the floor with a knife at her throat. I'd gone full black sun, the magic that seeped into everything in this world powering me up to new heights.

He seemed genuinely surprised that it was all a ruse to test my loyalty.

"That's not what the *shr'lei* were told," he explained. "We were led to believe it was true. Likely for good reason, which is why I'm going to keep it to myself."

"Did you know Hazel was here?"

"Yes, but I didn't know it was a secret." He shrugged. "It's none of my concern who the queen takes in as a ward. The crown has had an ongoing relationship with the Witches of your world for decades now, so it's not unusual."

Speaking of the queen… Rory and ignis had talked me down, but I was still annoyed about the afternoon's fake assassination attempt.

"Niarisshia ordered me to go into the city tomorrow. She wants to…" I sighed.

"She wants you seen," Altrys said. "I understand."

Niarisshia hoped parading me around would draw out the Chimera *and* my mother… if she still lived.

The last I knew of her—Aurae de Leiran—was in the vision I'd stumbled across in my dad's journal. He'd taken me from her arms the night I was born and conspired to bring me back to Earth.

They will covet her power for the rest of her life, she'd said.

"And we will protect her for the rest of ours," I whispered.

"Hmm?" Altrys asked.

"What if my mother is still alive?" I murmured. "If she reaches out…"

"You sound unhappy about it."

"I'm not, it's just… I wouldn't know what to say to her. She's a stranger to me. My father never spoke about her so all I know is the few scraps I picked out of his journal and the vile reputation of the de

Leirans. What if she's..." I couldn't manage to say it...*evil*.

"Agonising over what may or may not be will only cause you turmoil, Elspeth," Altrys said. "It's best not to dwell on the intangible."

"What is tangible is that I'm Unseelie and the one person alive who can trigger the apocalypse. People don't like Unseelie, but all that other stuff...? I'm afraid the entire city will riot if they see me. I know you said—"

Altrys cupped my face. "Elspeth, I will be with you. The *Shr'lei de Delei'an* don't escort Fae unless they are the queen. When they see us with you, they will know you hold the queen's favour."

A wave of exhaustion crashed into me. Tomorrow wasn't just a leisurely walk around the capital. There would be armoured guards, banners, and fanfare. La'luin would wake me up at the crack of dawn and dress me in some outlandish outfit, stick me on a horse, and bid me good luck.

Altrys sensed my unease and drew me into his lap. "Remember why you came here."

I nodded and traced my finger along his smooth jaw. "I miss this."

His brow knitted together. "My face?"

"Your scratchy beard."

"Sil Astrad has changed us both." He tucked a loose strand of emerald hair behind my ear. "What I wouldn't do to escape into the forest with you and leave the politics of this place behind."

"I think the same thing sometimes."

We fell silent, listening to the muffled sounds of the comings and goings in the palace outside the floor-to-ceiling windows.

Altrys's lips brushed against mine and his hands began to wander. "You do realise we are alone for the first time since we arrived?"

I wanted to throw myself at him, but the next step seemed to be fraught with a whole heap of baggage—which he deserved to know before we tore each other out of our clothes.

"Altrys…"

He drew back. "What's wrong?"

"I like having you here. I like this…" I held his face in my hand and pressed a light kiss on his lips. "But long term, I don't want a family. I won't bring children into this world if they have a chance of inheriting the de Leiran… *curse*. With what I am and what I'm destined to become, I can't offer you more than right now. This war with the Chimera… it might end with me dead or worse."

Altrys sighed and held me close. My heartbeat sped up and I began to have visions of him throwing me off his lap and storming out, never to be seen again. This was farther into a relationship as I'd ever been, and whatever happened next was unknown ground. I had to be prepared to enter broken heart territory or else.

Altrys was a man and a warrior. He was wise and strong. He was a thousand times removed from any of the boys I'd dated on Earth—immature morons who'd used me, then dumped me without so much as an explanation.

If Altrys didn't want me, then… Rory did, but it wasn't about love with him, not for me.

I began to tremble, anticipating the blow.

"Don't worry about children," Altrys said. "That is not an issue."

"What?"

"Elspeth, as a half-Shri'danann, half-De'ashlide, my curse runs deeper than only having paltry magic."

I blinked. "What do you mean?"

"I cannot have children."

"At all?"

"I am sterile."

I raised my eyebrows at his frankness. "Now I understand the assassins."

"And as for an after…" His gaze lowered. "As a *Shr'lei de Delei'an*, it is known that life comes with risk. My position offers death on a daily basis, so much so it is part of the oath we take. You saw the reality in Un Alari. If I were to die that day, I would have accepted it as my position dictates."

I believed him. It was as simple as that.

"Does it bother you?" I asked. "Not being able to…"

"No," he replied.

"Never?"

"Never. Strangely enough, it only seems to bother other people."

I smiled and my anxiety began to melt. "I'm sorry for making this a whole thing. I know we're not really… Well…"

"We're not really what?"

I shrugged, my cheeks heating. "Together. Committed. It's complicated, I get it."

"Elspeth, I am with you. There is no other. I understand what our lives are and what they will be."

"But—"

He placed a finger over my lips. "I don't know how it is where you come from, but here, we live for today. At least Fae like me do." He took a deep breath. "Why deny the pleasure of now because there may never be a tomorrow? No one knows the future. Not entirely. Visions can be changed, and prophecies are just poetry."

What Niarisshia had told me about actions being more important to her than words was becoming clearer. Perhaps that's why it always frustrated me when people did the opposite of what they said—I put too much faith in promises. Words held power, but actions told the real story.

I pushed the queen out of my mind and focused on Altrys.

"The pleasure of now?" I whispered, threading my fingers through his chocolate-coloured hair. "What does that entail exactly?"

His breath caught and he kissed me, his reply lost, but he didn't need words.

His actions told me everything I needed to know.

7

A scream echoing through my bedroom woke me with a start.

I sat up in bed, clutching the rumpled sheets against my chest, and my gaze met the reddening face of La'luin.

Altrys stirred next to me and he lifted his gaze just in time to catch the Fae fleeing for her life.

"Was that La'luin?" he rasped, his voice heavy with sleep.

I sighed. "The one and the only."

I was looking forward to waking up next to Altrys and pretending the world was far, far away for another hour at least. La'luin had put a stop to that.

"Your shoulder looks good." I traced the outline of the scars where the arrows had pierced his flesh. "You weren't lying about those healers."

"It's been three weeks," he murmured. "It's more than enough time to recover."

"Has it?" I counted in my head. Two weeks on the road, then a week in the capital. Well, a week and a day or two, but who was counting?

Altrys sat, the sheets falling away from his naked body. My gaze lowered.

"Do you like what you see?"

"You have a lot of scars." Adding to the arrow wounds was a slash on his side, a jagged cut on his upper left bicep, a puckered stab in his right thigh, various nicks here and there, and the chip on his jaw.

"Most of them are from training when I was young," he explained. "By the time we take our oaths, the *shr'lei* know if we can live up to our station or not by how many times we draw blood. The scars lessen significantly after that."

I frowned, understating more and more why all the *shr'lei* I'd met were hard, but Altrys wasn't paying any attention.

"I have to report to the citadel," he said then kissed me on the lips. "I will see you soon."

He dressed in a hurry, pulling on his boots and buttoning his shirt as he walked across the room.

"Altrys?"

He stopped and looked back, smiling as my cheeks heated.

"Yes," he replied, his gaze flowing over me, "I enjoyed myself. *Thoroughly*."

After breakfast, I was given the honour of the freedom to make my own way the citadel where the others were waiting for me.

I'd chosen the nicest clothing I could find that didn't involve skirts or frills and as La'luin eyed me from afar, I imagined her expression was one of begrudging acceptance. When she spotted my Druid's knife at my hip, all she did was sigh.

"Are you coming with us?" I asked.

"No, I have other duties to attend to today."

"Wow, the queen actually trusts me enough to let me out of your sight?"

"I didn't know," she murmured, tugging me close. "You must accept my apology. I would never—"

"La'luin," I said, interrupting her, "I believe you."

Her expression melted and her eyes widened. "You do?"

"Of course, I do."

The Fae smiled and let me go. "The *Shr'lei de Delei'an* will guide you through the city. Altrys knows the city well—he will be able to answer any question you may have."

Two *shr'lei* were standing with Rory by the gates and four saddled horses were tethered nearby. The Druid spotted me, said something to the Fae, then mounted his horse.

One *shr'lei* was Altrys, and the other was Elion. The men wore smart leather and steel-plated armour emblazoned with the *tuathade'shri* on their chests. They carried swords on their backs, their waist-length decorative silver and gold cloaks pinned to the side to allow quick access to their weapons if things went sideways. I admired the scaled leather that travelled the length of their left arms, but their right—both Fae's dominant hands—was free apart from simple leather guards clasped around their forearms. They also wore scaled trousers and knee-high boots. It was far from ceremonial garb, but it got the message across. There was no mistaking them as anything but *Shr'lei de Delei'an.*

Elion looked up when Altrys nodded towards me. He didn't seem thrilled, but I suspected he wasn't accustomed to babysitting duty.

"It's nice to see you again, Elion," I told him.

He gave me a sharp bow and gestured to the grey horse beside Rory's. "I thought you might prefer a mount you are familiar with."

I smiled. *"A'ladrei."*

Rory eyed me suspiciously as I mounted my horse and handed me a mossy-green bag containing Ignis in kitten form.

"What's that look for?" I asked.

"La'luin is having a breakdown," Rory told me with a sigh. "She was so worked up, I just had to ask."

"The Fae are supposed to be open about these things," I grumbled, arranging Ignis on the saddle in front of me. "I don't know why she's so bothered."

"So, you and Altrys…" Rory shifted in his saddle and the leather creaked. "It's really a thing?"

He was still asking, which didn't bode well. Nothing had changed my opinion about having a family, and Rory wanted children along with the romance. It was such a Druid thing to nurture life and continue bloodlines, but mine had to end with me. The Odhweine name would fade, but the de Leiran curse would never rise again.

Still, my feelings for Altrys had little to do with his inability to become a father.

"I'd like it to be a thing," I replied, wanting to be honest. "But right now… There's a lot going on."

"Ignis wanted to come," the Druid said, changing the subject so fast I almost got whiplash. "I told him it'd better be in miniature form. There's going to be enough eyes on us without a black and blue magical tiger wandering down the main street."

I placed my palm on the lump in the bag and nodded.

Elion marched over to us and checked our horses tack like he hadn't seen me take care of it for two weeks straight.

"Altrys?" he called.

"The way is ready," he replied.

Elion turned to me and Rory. "Lor'Odhweine?"

I raised my eyebrows at his formal, and over-respectful, address. "I'm ready when you are."

Rory shot me a look and I rolled my eyes as the *shr'lei* mounted their horses and the group moved forwards.

The gates opened, dragging back on heavy hinges.

My first introduction into the world of the Druids was one of secrecy. On Earth, especially while the Chimera hunted us, it meant life or death. It was a fine line here, but now we could be open. The queen had allied herself with us—only while it suited her—but it was up to us to show the Fae we were good people. Rory was a true Druid, peaceful and wise… but I was still the *Liash li Ashli*. Passing through the gates seemed like the beginning of a new chapter, and one I wasn't sure I wanted to read.

Sil Astrad was certainly a beautiful city. On first glance, I had the same impression of it as I did the day we'd arrived.

Trees were left to grow wherever they'd sprouted —which seemed to be generations ago in some cases —and their branches twisted and turned, creating homes for birds and other creatures, which were allowed to roam free. The roads were winding and rarely ran straight because of this, but it added to the magical charm of the city.

As our small party rode past shops and houses, Fae stopped to see who the *Shr'lei de Delei'an* were escorting. They craned their necks and leaned out of windows, but when they say my green hair, then began to whisper. Some turned away, while others stared openly. Few seemed to be impressed by my supposed heroics with the queen, but it was only what I could see on the surface.

What I did notice was that almost everyone we

passed were Shri'danann. Many were Seelie with warm-coloured hair—reds, oranges, yellows, and pinks—but I was drawn to the few Unseelie, my gaze looking for the same emerald green that coloured my own locks.

Aurae de Leiran. I tried to imagine what it would mean if she'd been here this whole time. The best place for someone to hide was in the middle of it all, underneath the candle where the shadow is at its darkest—the last place anyone would think to look.

Altrys and Elion led us through the streets, telling me and Rory about the history of the city and how it was founded over three thousand years ago by the Tuatha de Danann. It was their capital, and ruined in many wars, until the reformation. In recent years, it was the site where Queen Aibell oversaw a treaty between the Seelie and Unseelie, ending the civil war between the two Shri'danann clans, bringing peace to the realms and the city of Sil Astrad.

I vaguely remembered La'luin telling me the treaty was on display in the library in Lor As'tuann, but I hadn't seen it in person yet.

We toured the rest of the markets, sampling food and goods made by different trades. Rory stopped at a shop selling crystals, drawn by the energy in the display on a table outside. His Colour vibrated so hard, even I felt it as he ran his fingers over each and every point.

The harbour was next, the various tall ships a

sight out of Earth's history books. Technology had advanced so differently here—the adage of magic rendering things like electricity and mechanics obsolete. The Fae simply saw no point creating machines, and I doubted they'd see them as more than monsters that devoured nature in order to operate.

I'd never thought much about it before awakening as a Druid, but I understood nature in a way most humans didn't. When you felt the organic life force of the planet and the effects of the modern world, it was difficult not to.

I stroked my palm over my horse's neck and looked around at the sailors loading crates onto a vessel named the *Ad Fralei*. They were all De'ashlide, but the men who seemed to be calling the shots were Shri'danann.

It wasn't the first time I'd noticed the divide between Fae, and it wouldn't be the last.

"Remember what you told me the day I arrived here?" I asked Rory.

Following my gaze to the ship, he asked, "Which part?"

"The divide."

"Ah." He nodded and glanced at Altrys and Elion.

"It's not helpful," I muttered. "We're being seen, but…"

'It's not the entire story,' Ignis said. He'd been watching our progress from inside the bag, his head peeking out just enough so he could see.

'No,' I replied. '*It's a curated tour. One slanted towards the Shri'danann.*'

"Prejudice doesn't simply stop because of a treaty," Rory murmured. "It's deeper than that."

"I feel like…" My heart grew heavy. "I have a decision to make. One I thought I'd already…"

'It's okay,' Ignis told me. '*You need to make peace with the reality of your prophecy, Elspeth.*'

"I agree," Rory said.

I looked at him with raised eyebrows.

The Druid smirked. "The cat can multi-task now."

'*I learn fast.*'

Snorting, I turned to Altrys and Elion and waved them over. I knew there was an ulterior royal motive behind this day trip, but it was time to do something about the biased babysitting.

"This tour has been lovely," I said to the men, "but it's not the true face of Sil Astrad."

"Lor'Odhweine," Elion began, and I sighed.

"Stop it with the pleasantries, Elion. My name is Elspeth, not Lor'whatever. I don't have a title in this world, and I don't need one. I would prefer not being put on a pedestal."

The *Shr'lei* scowled and nodded. "As you wish." Then he moved away, edging his horse along the quayside.

I looked at Altrys. "Shall we go down the road less travelled?"

He squirmed in his saddle. "Elspeth, we have orders."

"I want to understand the world I've pledged to save," I told him. "I care about you, Altrys, but I don't care one iota about your orders."

Rory snorted, earning himself a wary glance from Altrys.

"Elspeth," Elion called out, "I think we best continue on."

"If I'm making you uncomfortable, Elion, you're free to go back to the citadel," I told him. "I'm not following your pre-approved tour anymore."

I spurred the horse on and we left the harbour, joining the traffic into the marketplace where I took a left instead of a right.

Behind me, I heard the *Shr'lei* arguing in Fae, then the rumble of hooves as Rory and Altrys caught up with me.

"Elion is angry," the Fae told me. "He won't let this go."

"I hope I won't get you into trouble," I said, "but this is important."

I allowed my horse to wander through the De'ashlide market, watching the people and stalls as we passed. It was bleaker here, the brightly painted houses were replaced with white and brown, the shops weren't as lavish—they sold more practical items like fruits and vegetables, basic breads, meat, tools, and clothing.

I saw two Shri'danann, but they were both Unseelie and kept their hair mostly covered. I felt like we were in a Harry Potter novel and had taken a wrong turn in Diagon Alley. The air was different, but not evil or dark. It was the air of simple reality.

A commotion drew my attention away from the market and I steered the horse towards the sound. Rory was behind me while Altrys lingered farther back, watching the flow of Fae like a hawk.

Ahead, a De'ashlide girl lay in the mud, covering her face as three Unseelie Shri'danann boys threw rocks and insults at her. As the stones hit her arms, they popped with magic, leaving red marks on her skin. She cried out in pain as one whacked her on the nose.

They didn't seem that old, either—about eight or nine.

In that moment, I saw myself in the little girl. *Make yourself tiny, Elspeth, so you're not big enough to become a target.* It never worked, though. The smaller I became, the harder the bullies came down on me and the worse it hurt. I still paid the price, all these years later, even after all the battles I'd fought.

Throwing my leg over my horse, I slid from the saddle and landed with a thud on the road.

The market fell into a charged hush as I walked towards the children, but I wasn't paying much attention. Behind me, I heard Altrys call out and I held up my hand to silence him.

"What's going on here?" I asked, raising my voice.

The Shri'danann boys turned, and when they saw me, their eyes widened in fear. They cried out in Fae and scattered, darting between stalls and pushing over startled passersby, leaving the girl crying in the dirt.

I looked down at her with a sigh and held out my hand. "Are you all right?"

The girl wiped her nose, leaving a smear of red on the back of her sleeve. She looked up at me and scowled.

"*Unseelie za'adei,*" she hissed.

It was something foul, that much was clear from the gasps from the crowd.

My power simmered, taunting me from beyond the veil and I scowled down at her. She scrambled to her feet and took off, pushing through the onlookers and disappearing like a mouse scurrying into a crack in the wall.

Rory stood beside me and offered me a sympathetic pat on my shoulder.

"If you wanted to make a scene, you certainly delivered," he murmured.

"I didn't want to make a scene," I shot back. "I wanted to *help*."

"I know, but I don't think she wanted it."

"It's not about wanting it," Altrys said, standing on my other side. "It's about your privilege."

I scowled and looked around at the market. Fae were hurrying away now, keeping their gazes anywhere but on us.

"We're outsiders," Rory said. "The De'ashlide don't want our pity. They just want to be equal. All we can do is treat others the way we want to be treated and let them shine on their own terms... instead of pushing them back down." Spoken like a true Druid.

The girl was long gone, but my mind weighed heavy. "Can we do anything for her?"

Altrys shook his head. "You can't change four thousand years of—"

"Four thousand years?" I exclaimed.

What kind of world was I trying to save? Was the one the Chimera trying to create any different? Was protecting the Earth any different? The choice seemed clear—save the world—but was it worth it?

"Elspeth," Altrys said, tugging on my arm.

"It's not fair," I whispered.

"No, it's not," he replied, "but we should leave."

I sniffed and studied the faces passing by. They didn't want us here, least of all me. These were people who feared Shri'danann and the kind of justice they handed out. Not all magical Fae were the same, but this wasn't Un Alari... and I was the *Liash li Ashli*. What I symbolised was worse.

"You're here to stop the Chimera," Rory said, "not champion social reform. There's only so much you can do."

Altrys nodded. "By saving our world, you give us all a chance to become wiser."

He knew a great deal about the prejudice of the

Shri'danann. Altrys had to fight for everything in his life, especially his position as a *Shr'lei de Delei'an*.

'*He is wise,*' Ignis told me as I climbed back onto my horse. '*He has suffered because of his birth but chooses to see past the hate. He has tried to bring the two realities together in his own way.*'

'*Perhaps we need more of that,*' I mused. '*Everyone doing a little is better than no one doing nothing at all.*'

'*Hope and opportunity are powerful things,*' the cat added as I allowed Altrys to lead us back to the main road where Elion waited. '*Rory and Altrys are both right.*'

'*I trust them. It's just the pressure is mounting. Hidden away in Lor As'tuann, I almost forgot the reality of what's coming. Out here, the world is so… raw.*'

'*Earth is the same,*' Ignis said, wiggling in my bag. '*Don't let the ugly outshine the good. There are so many beautiful things about this world that are worth protecting, too.*'

I smiled as we rode away from the marketplace, remembering the weeks on the road with Altrys and the *Shr'lei de Delei'an*. Even the Un Alari guard rated a mention. I thought about the different landscapes— the valleys of Lith'lander and the Silver Mountains— and even the elementals I'd seen in the forest. Magic was only one part of this world, and it was a gift. The Shri'danann should treat it with more respect.

'*Beautiful,*' Ignis stated.

'*You saw that?*' I asked.

'*I did.*'

Hope. Was that what I was fighting for? No, not quite. It was a part of it, but it was deeper than that.

Choice, I decided. The opportunity for these people to choose to become whoever they wanted to be.

Choice, hope, opportunity.

Powerful things, indeed.

8

———

After that day, I began to find an inner peace with the turmoil I felt with my unpredictable future.

I listened more to La'luin and helped Rory with his portals, learning everything I could, and Ignis continued to roam, adding to our knowledge of palace gossip. If there was something to be heard, he managed to get back to us unseen.

We'd been alternating days in the city with my training and Rory's research, but never in a predictable pattern. News of my adventures were spreading through both Shri'danann and De'ashlide neighbourhoods, but not all the feedback was five stars.

I had a reputation forged in a prophecy of destruction and the Fae feared the Chimera. They'd heard stories about their secret agents and the threat of war was a sore point for many. The civil war had ended less than thirty years ago, and no one was thrilled about returning to those dreadful days.

Altrys began teaching me how to use a sword, the weight unfamiliar and betraying my lack of upper body strength. It didn't help my confidence when we began attracting an audience. The shr'lei were just as curious as the bravest Fae in the city. They all wanted a good look at the creature who held the fate of the world in her hands.

I learned how to parry and strike, the sword becoming an extension of my arm. Altrys spent more time explaining how to read my opponent than I did with an actual blade in my hand, but I let him do his thing without complaint. He was a member of the queen's elite guard after all.

Soon my arm ached less and less, and so did my rear end after a day of riding in Sil Astrad. I was becoming stronger in both body and mind, and I often wondered what my father would think if he saw me now. Waging war and saving worlds was quite literally universes away from the hopes I'd had of following in his footsteps as an environmental scientist.

Ignis joined us on all our outings, working on his voice and offering his insight wherever we went. Most of them had to do with food, but his range was extending to include Rory, Altrys, and Elion all at once.

Speaking of Elion, he'd begrudgingly accepted he had no control over me, but there hadn't been any more encounters like the one in the marketplace on our first trip. I'd kept my mouth closed when it came to hot topics, but held my head high, talking to anyone who showed interest.

I even grilled Elion about the customs and gossip of the city whenever Ignis wasn't showering us with his insightful opinions about whatever scent caught his fancy.

Life was tense, but I considered it a time of preparation. It kept my mind off what was coming, and I managed to forget why we were here… until everything changed.

It was one morning, a month after the day in the marketplace, when the news came.

Altrys and I were going through swordplay drills at the citadel when he abruptly stopped. I pulled back my wooden practice sword with a jerk, narrowly missing whacking him on the head.

"What?" I asked, scowling. "Don't do that. I almost knocked you out."

"A messenger comes," he replied, wiping the sweat off his brow. "And you could never knock me out."

I ignored the last part. "A messenger?"

"Lor'Odhweine?" A male voice echoed behind me. "I have a message for you, if you please."

I sighed and turned around. I really wished they'd stop calling me that. The messenger was a young boy, perhaps seventeen or eighteen years of age. When my gaze met his, he faltered.

"Yes?" I prodded.

"Q-queen Niarisshia requests y-your im-immediate presence," he replied, haltingly. He glanced at Altrys and I swore the boy broke out into a cold sweat. "A-altrys, *Shr'lei de Delei'an*, y-you are to a-accompany her."

Altrys put the wooden sword back onto the rack. "And where is this meeting taking place?"

The messenger flushed scarlet. "T-the c-council chambers."

I shot a look at Altrys, who just shook his head with an amused smile. "That will be all," he told the boy, who scurried away like a frightened mouse.

"That was awkward," I drawled, putting my practice sword back.

"He was intimidated by you," Altrys told me. "Your reputation is growing, Lor'Odhweine."

I shoved him. "Shut up. He pissed his pants when you looked at him."

"That's because I already have a reputation."

Shaking my head, I asked, "What do you suppose the queen wants?"

"It could be anything."

I froze. "Do you think she has news about my mother?"

"There is only one way to find out."

"Wait..." I sniffed my shirt. "I can't go see the queen smelling like this."

Did I have time to go past my rooms? The palace was like a maze, so probably not... Unless...

"Elspeth, she said immediate," Altrys said.

"So?" I grabbed his hand and phased for the first time since arriving in the Fae realm.

We disappeared from the citadel training yard and appeared in my bedroom in the blink of an eye. The responsiveness of my power sent shivers down my spine and I grinned. *Wow.*

Altrys stumbled, his face pale, and he muttered something in Fae that didn't sound like it was fit for delicate ears.

"Sorry." I grimaced. "I should have warned you."

He wiped his brow. "It would have been appropriate."

"Give me a minute to change, then we can pop over the hall and get you one of Rory's shirts."

"Elspeth—"

"It'll be fine," I called out as I rummaged through the rack of clothing. "He won't mind."

Our journey to the council chambers was a longer affair. I hadn't seen it before, so we had to make the trek through the twisting corridors of Lor As'tuann the old-fashioned way. Altrys wasn't keen on phasing again and was relieved when I explained how my power worked.

When we arrived, I was expecting to see a small room with a table and chairs, but the Fae equivalent of a conference room was a great deal more elaborate than a barren space with a whiteboard and an espresso machine.

A council meeting in these parts comprised of tiered seating for a hundred on natural mahogany carved chairs padded with elaborate silver and gold-starred fabric. Banners emblazoned with the royal *tuathade'shri* hung around the room and jewelled garlands and crests were mounted on the head of each seat. I gathered they signified various families and houses in the Fae nobility who had a place at council, but today they were empty.

At the head of the room was a throne much like the one the Lor'andann of Un Alari had, though the head of this one was carved with an intricate pattern of stars, and in the centre was a large *tuathade'shri* made out of pure diamond—I could feel the reverberation of it from the door and knew it was more than a fancy decoration.

The queen was protected at all times, which made her fake assassination even more infuriating to me. People had believed it so easily.

These chambers were where the reigning monarch held 'court' with the leaders of their kingdom—which meant this meeting was official, and not some paltry little progress report.

Something had happened. Either the Chimera had revealed their hand or… What if they'd found Aurae de Leiran? I wanted to know my mother my entire life, but now… I wasn't so sure I wanted to.

My heart twisted as I realised I was afraid.

The throne was empty, but there was no mistaking Niarisshia. She sat at the head of a long mahogany table in the centre of the room, her presence radiating.

I'd never once seen her wear a crown or any item to symbolise her rule—she didn't need them—but today she wore a delicate necklace around her pale neck. The silver chain carried a simple diamond pendant that sparkled like a star in the night sky. The longer I peered at it, the more my power recoiled. Looking up, her gaze met mine and her lips curved into a knowing smile.

She had a way to protect herself from the black sun. I couldn't say I was surprised. Her blood was different than anyone I'd ever met.

Rory and Ignis were already seated at the opposite end of the table to the queen. The cat was in his tiger shape, his eyes sparkling blue.

"Welcome, Elspeth," Niarisshia said. "Altrys. Please, take a seat."

I chose to sit next to Rory and Altrys took the seat next to mine. It seemed improper to be anywhere near the queen, but I wasn't complaining.

Once we'd settled, the Lor As'tuann guards closed the doors, the boom echoing through the near-empty chamber.

Rory glared at Altrys but addressed me. "Is he wearing my shirt?"

Niarisshia folded her hands in her lap, her slight movement commanding our attention. "Yesterday evening, I received a message from Aurae de Leiran."

She said it so blandly, it took a moment for it to sink in.

"My mother is alive?" I gasped. "Truly?"

"*Allegedly*," she replied coolly.

My heart twisted and my hands began to shake. I shoved them underneath the table and swallowed hard.

Niarisshia looked at me, her gaze so piercing I imagined she could see into my soul.

"Don't fall silent, Elspeth," she said. "You have been so forthcoming until now."

Was she goading me? I reached out to Ignis for comfort, his prisms shimmering as I threaded my fingers through the shaggy hair on his neck.

'*Do not be afraid,*' he told me. '*She needs you more than you need her.*'

I gathered my courage and thought of my father and Delilah—both wise leaders—and tried to channel them.

"Why would she contact you so openly?" I asked. "It doesn't feel right. Why wouldn't the message come to me directly?"

"Perhaps she knew there was no other way to contact you," Altrys offered. "Any message coming to Lor As'tuann would be stopped and any friends she had before she went into hiding would be long gone."

"Or this is a trap," Rory stated.

"Precisely." Niarisshia smiled at the Druid. "There

are nuances to our kind that you are unfamiliar with, Elspeth. The Fae can be blunt and do not take kindly to lies, but on the other side of the coin, the truth can be twisted with illusion to create a new truth."

That was what made the Chimera such a threat, I thought. *Truth could be changed if enough people believed in the lie.*

"It was what drove our people to civil war," she continued, her eyes darkening. "The Unseelie are prone to illusions… which is just a pretty word for lying."

Seriously. I held my tongue while my anger simmered. I was Unseelie, my family was evil and twisted Unseelie, but I was also a Druid. I was my father's daughter and knew nothing of the de Leiran legacy I carried, but the queen knew this.

"This isn't about the past," I said, once my veins had cooled. "This is about the future."

"And what future is that?" Niarisshia glared. "If you have a strategy my generals, Lor'andann's, and advisors haven't considered, please share them with me."

"The only path forwards is this woman," I said. "We must speak with her. If the story I know about her is true, then the Chimera hunted her as ruthlessly as they have me and the Druids. I can force her truth if she is who she says she is…"

"How so?"

"With my power," I explained. "All are judged before they cross the veil."

"Is that so?" Her slender fingers moved to the diamond around her neck.

"My queen, if I may," Altrys said. "Time is short, and I have a recommendation that may please everyone."

She nodded. "What is your proposal, Altrys, *Shr'lei de Delei'an?*"

"If this is our only lead, then we should take it, but only a small group should go to mitigate the risk of being captured or discovered by the Chimera. If the woman is indeed Aurae de Leiran, then a subtle presence may be the better approach. Armoured soldiers and a detachment of *shr'lei* may only serve to frighten her back into hiding." He glanced at me fleetingly before returning his gaze to the queen. "She is expecting to see Elspeth, so she must go. I am familiar with the powers of the *Liash li Ashli* and will not falter if she needs to use them in battle. I would offer myself to accompany her if it pleases you."

"I want to go," Rory interrupted. "It's important that I stay beside Elspeth."

"The Chimera hunt you for your power," Niarisshia stated, her eyes narrowing. "It would be reckless."

"On Earth, they were able to track us when we used our power," Rory explained. "They know we are in Sil Astrad, but they won't know we've left unless we use our Colour. With all due respect, I've lived my entire life fighting them. They murdered my parents and took the lives of many others, Elspeth's father included. I have to see this through."

I cleared my throat. "Rory and I are a package deal. Together as Druids, our Colour is stronger and it has only helped us in the past."

"I propose we leave at first light."

Niarisshia leaned back in her chair, her magic pulsing as she considered Altrys's proposal.

"It is quite the battalion you have formed around yourself, Elspeth," she said. Her gaze moved from Altrys to me then back again.

Mine and Altrys's relationship wasn't a secret, but we didn't flaunt it. In comparison to Earth, the Fae were quite progressive about sexual relationships between different Fae races, until it became about procreation. Whatever Niarisshia thought about it was a mystery.

"We are the same," I corrected her. "No one is above the other."

Silence fell, the length of table between us stretching even farther.

"Altrys, report to Ilbryen in the citadel," Niarisshia commanded, breaking the ice. "He will inform you of the details."

He rose and bowed low. "At once, my queen."

"Elspeth, Raurich," her gaze lowered to Ignis, "and… *companion*, no doubt you have preparations to make for your journey. It is a hard road, and a long one. The morning awaits." She gestured to the doors. "Do what you must."

We stood and I was about to let out a sigh of relief when Niarisshia's voice rang out once more. "Elspeth."

I turned and our gazes met.

"I have put my trust in you, but do not be fooled."

I felt Rory look at me as I nodded. I understood. Trust was taken away easier than it was given. If it looked like I was going to turn to the dark and fulfil the prophecy in the name of the Chimera, then they would kill me. And by they, I meant Altrys.

Niarisshia smiled, but the warmth never reached her eyes. Schooling my expression to nothingness, I turned and strode out of the chamber, Rory and Ignis following close behind.

La'luin was waiting for us when we left the council chambers.

Altrys and Rory left us, both needing to make preparations for tomorrow's departure.

We walked down the hall away from the guards posted at the doors and I stopped, my thoughts troubled. There was always an ulterior motive when it came to Niarisshia. None of my encounters with her had been on a level playing field and this one was no different. In fact, it felt worse.

'Be careful,' Ignis said, feeling the restrained chaos of my thoughts.

"She allowed Altrys to come with us so easily," I said. "Why?"

"The queen allows it because he is... He..." La'luin's cheeks heated.

"Expendable," I finished for her.

'Elspeth,' Ignis prodded.

Altrys shouldn't exist. A De'ashlide with magic, no matter how little, was dangerous. Then why did they allow him to become a *shr'lei* in the first place? So they could control him? Why did Niarisshia grant him permission to come with me and Rory to meet my mother?

Because if he died in pursuit of the Chimera, it wouldn't be any great loss. His memory would be a beacon of hope for the De'ashlide, and a notch on Niarisshia's political belt and help solidify her hold on power. The people would love her for her inclusiveness and Altrys would be a symbolic martyr.

And if he needed to kill me, despite how he felt about it, he would be a hero that bridged the gap between all Fae. The De'ashlide half-blood who took out the *Liash li Ashli* and saved the world.

Was Niarisshia just playing the game to appease all sides? I couldn't tell. The mystery of her heart was a closed door to all but her. Good, bad, or in-between, she was simply the queen.

'Her motives are her own,' Ignis told me. *'We watch for treachery, but I don't think she is planning to double-cross you. Perhaps she is simply covering all scenarios.'*

"It's not like that," La'luin said, unable to hear Ignis's commentary. "Altrys is a highly respected *Shr'lei de Delei'an*. He has done much in the service of the queen and much for the De'ashlide. It's just politics,

Elspeth. She has to remain impartial to her personal feelings."

Harsh, but fair. That was Skye's assessment of Niarisshia and it was pretty spot on, but it didn't make it hurt any less when that impartialness was made at the expense of someone I cared about.

But if I knew Altrys as well as I thought I did, he already knew and understood what this journey meant… and if I asked him about it, he wouldn't lie.

Perhaps it was best not to bring it up at all.

"Come," La'luin said. "Enough about those things. I will help you pack for your journey. Will Ignis be joining you?"

"Yes," I muttered, glancing back at the council chamber doors. "He is."

"That's a shame," the Fae said. "I do enjoy his company."

'*She is pretty*,' Ignis said to me. '*Don't you think?*'

9

Dawn found my shivering back in the courtyard of the *shr'lei* citadel the following morning.

A frost had settled on every available surface overnight, a bleak omen for the journey we were about to undertake, or at least it felt that way.

I pulled a pair of gloves over my freezing hands. The insides were lined with a knitted, soft spun wool that was warm and silky to the touch. Fine garments for any person.

Altrys was marching around, giving orders to the servants who were packing our horses. Finally, he shooed them away and checked the tack himself.

"The weather has been fine this whole time and now it wants to dump ice on us?" Rory complained, standing beside me.

He wore hardy riding clothes, much the same as Altrys, and looked nothing like the roguish Scotsman I'd met almost a year ago in Edinburgh. Had it been that long? Maybe it was less than that. I'd lost all track of time since landing headfirst into the supernatural world.

"The mountains will be colder," I replied as Ignis sat at my feet. "You'll be thankful for the cloaks and extra socks La'luin made us pack when we go up in altitude."

"Scots can do highlands," the Druid replied. "You were raised in Australia, so I'm more worried about you."

I snorted and punched him playfully on the arm. "It's not all tropical oasis, you know."

"All I'm saying is that the meeting could have been somewhere by a beach and palm tree." I knew what he meant. The message proposed a meeting in a small village near the northeastern reaches of the kingdom. At midnight, a week from now, amongst the ancient *lor'ashlar*.

With no way to reply to the missive, we only had once option. Show up.

"*Tha mi an dòchas gum bi tìde gu leòr againn,*" he said in Gaelic as Altrys approached, carrying a long bundle in his arms.

"It's enough," I told him. "We've only lost one day to debating."

Rory sighed and eyed the Fae. "I was talking about the beach."

"The horses are ready," Altrys said, his breath vaporising on the chilly air. "This is for you." He held out the bundle towards me and I flushed, glad the cold dawn had already made my cheeks pink.

I took it from him, surprised to find it was heavy. "Is this what I think it is?"

The *Shr'lei* smiled. "Unwrap it and see."

It was a small blade, about two-thirds the length of a standard sword, but the same as Altrys carried—the standard *shr'lei* issue—but it seemed to be more elaborately forged. The scabbard was plain brown leather, attached to a long belt with a steel buckle.

The hilt was made up of three different components. The grip was wrapped in hard leather and fit my hand well. The cross-guard was comprised of twisted steel, gold, and silver. And the pommel was a flat steel circle imbedded with clear quartz crystal with an obsidian and gold vein through the centre.

Sliding the sword out of the scabbard, my breath caught as I made out the flowing script of the Fae travelling down the centre, beginning at the hilt and down towards the tip. Around the writing, an intricate filigree pattern worked its way outwards, fading as it reached the sharp edges.

The sword was beautiful, but it wasn't made for a glass display case. It was meant to be used and used well, and from the marks along the blade's edge, I hadn't been the first owner.

"Altrys..." I looked up at him. "Are you sure you want to give this to me?"

He nodded. "You have your Druid's knife with its

prayer, so it is only fair you have something fitting to honour your Fae blood."

I ran my gloved finger over the script. "What does it say?"

"*Ashlar an lor, shride lei an val'ash,*" Altrys murmured. "Honour the dead, for they give us life."

"Where's my sword?" Rory asked, his eyes narrowing.

I bit my tongue as Altrys's smile faded, then he pointed to Rory's horse. "There is a weapon with your belongings, Druid."

Rory said nothing and walked away. As soon as he was past Altrys, he turned and pulled a face, mocking the Fae.

I sighed and slipped the blade back into the scabbard.

"Here," Altrys said. "Let me fasten it for you. This strap is fashioned to be worn over your back."

"Just like we've been practicing," I said as he pushed my cloak over my shoulder.

He smiled as he eased the sword over my head, positioning it on my back. Finally, he fastened the belt into the buckle, the leather laying snuggly between my breasts. His fingers lingered a little longer that was needed, and he smiled.

"How does that feel?"

"Good," I murmured, catching his silver gaze.

"Oh, there you are!" The sound of La'luin's voice echoed across the courtyard and we turned as she hurried towards us, her orange hair in disarray and a bundle in her arms. "I thought I might miss you."

"Is all well, *Li'deshri?*" Altrys enquired.

"Yes, I dearly wanted to make sure you departed with all you needed," she replied, handing me a fur-lined bag. "For Ignis… I know he likes to travel as a kitten."

'*I do,*' Ignis told her. Even though he had a voice, he rarely seemed to use it. Sometimes he was so silent, I forgot he was there.

"Thank you, La'luin," I said, opening the bag as Ignis began to manipulate his prisms.

The tiger shook his coat, his fur sparkling and within a few shakes, he was small enough to fit inside. He mewled, his tabby coat settling into its new shape, and jumped into the bag.

'*Perfect,*' he said. '*Thank you, La'luin.*'

"What will happen once we're gone?" I slung the strap of the bag over my shoulder. "The Chimera are watching. I'm worried…"

"Don't worry," she said. "There will still be sightings of the *Liash li Ashli* in the city. They won't know you've even left."

I raised my eyebrows. "I have a body double?"

La'luin nodded. "An illusion, but one even the Chimera would be hard-pressed to see through."

"Niarisshia's really thought of everything, hasn't she?"

The Fae frowned. "I wouldn't let her hear you refer to her by her personal name."

I snorted. "I wouldn't dream of it."

La'luin smelled and reached over my shoulders. Pulling up my hood, she tucked my green braid inside the fabric. "As they say in your world, good luck, Elspeth Odhweine. I hope you find your mother and she is everything you've been hoping for."

"Thank you," I replied, my heart lurching at the thought. "Me, too."

***

Three solitary figures rode away from Sil Astrad under the cover of fog.

I huddled underneath my cloak, the hilt of my new sword poking over my left shoulder. Ignis was curled up inside his fur-lined bag between my legs on my saddle, toasty warm and oblivious to the ice numbing my toes despite my thick woollen socks.

Mist shrouded the entire landscape, gathering in every dip it could find. Glancing over my shoulder, the warm lights of the capital blurred into a haze and the rising sun hovered on the horizon, barely strong enough to break through. Even the ocean was invisible.

It reminded me of death.

I turned back around, the reins creaking in my stiff hands. Altrys led the way as he was familiar with the roads, and Rory rode beside me, his horse plodding along at a mediocre rate.

The fog cleared by mid-morning, and the sun

warmed our backs as the road began to fill with people moving towards the capital. We passed everything from horse-drawn caravans, wagons full of goods for the markets, and travelling Fae on foot. A detachment of soldiers passed us, trotting at a steady pace, but they never looked twice at us.

I kept my hood up, watching with curious eyes as the farmland surrounding the walls of Sil Astrad gave way to woodlands that stretched into wilderness. On the horizon, I could make out the faint purplish smudge of the mountain range we were headed towards.

Altrys said the range was called An Valran, meaning the White Pinnacles—not to be confused with Ad Valrah, the Iron Pinnacle where Altrys and I had been before.

The population was sparse there, as even the smallest peaks rose higher than the ones around Un Alari. Winters were harsh and dangerous, and summers were just as unpredictable. Landslides from thawing ice and snow had made their disastrous mark throughout history, like a snowy Fae version of Pompeii. Many cities had been buried under mud and permafrost, but people still settled in the area. The largest settlement was the village of Lir Cael, which was where the meeting with the woman claiming to be my mother, Aurae de Leiran, would take place.

The first night we set up camp in a secluded clearing at least a hundred metres from the road. Our fire would cast light, but not enough to draw attention from unwanted eyes, and the surrounding woodland would shield us from the wind and the frost which we knew would come again in the morning.

Altrys spirited away into the forest searching for dinner while Rory and I tended to the horses and got a fire going.

The Druid dumped an armful of fallen branches in the centre of the clearing, his gaze going to the Fae more than it stayed on his work.

"You need to give it a rest," I said as I arranged the twigs and tinder I'd collected. "Remember what we're here for, Rory."

"I can't help it," he replied. "Does he know I'm a vegetarian?"

"Yes, you can," I shot back. "And there are plenty of things for you to eat."

Ignis wriggled out of his bag and shook, growing to the size of a large house cat.

'Don't let your jealousy blind you,' he told the Druid. *'The Chimera will be watching.'* Ignis then leapt up into a tree and began to tear apart the bark with his claws.

"How can I take the cat seriously when he does stuff like that?" Rory muttered, lighting the fire. He blew on the tiny flame and it caught, whooshing as it latched onto the wood.

"It's a side effect of his prisms," I replied. "It's got nothing to do with his soul."

Altrys wasn't long in returning. He carried two creatures that looked a lot like rabbits, and a small bag which contained a selection of wild plants—mushrooms, vegetables, roots, and nuts.

He was used to doing all the work from his years of travelling alone, and he said nothing as he began to prepare a thick stew in one pot and another vegetarian dish in another.

I shot Rory a meaningful glare and he shrugged.

"It's become so cold so fast, even by the ocean," I said, warming my hands by the fire.

"The seasons are changing," Altrys told us. "It is not a good time to be travelling to the mountains."

"Which is why the message came now, I suppose," I muttered.

"Is it normal for the weather to change so much in the span of a day?" Rory asked. "The seasons change gradually on Earth."

Altrys nodded. "They can."

"How long does summer last?" I wondered.

"Our seasons last a whole year before changing," the Fae replied.

Rory looked at me, his brow furrowed. "I thought we were in a parallel universe."

"It's not an exact copy," I told him. "One little microbe can change the course of an entire world's evolution. Remember that hell dimension?"

"Please don't remind me." He lowered his gaze and dug his spoon into the vegetable pot and stirred.

Altrys listened to our exchange with interest. "You speak of the strangest things. I wonder if I would like your world."

"It's overrated," I drawled.

'It is much like mine,' Ignis said, pawing at Altrys's leg.

"Do you miss it?" the Fae asked as he handed the cat a piece of rabbit.

I looked into the fire. "I miss… I miss the Warren. I miss Delilah and the Elders. I miss Jaimie. I even miss Darby and Vanora."

Rory snorted. "You miss Vanora?"

"Don't you?"

He sighed and resumed stirring, not wanting to discuss her. "I miss Edinburgh, but I made a *gealladh.*"

"What does that mean?" Altrys asked.

Rory looked up at the Fae, his shoulders tense. "It means promise."

Altrys seemed to understand that Rory wasn't going to elaborate. He didn't seem bothered by it, he just checked on the stew and brushed his hands on his trousers.

"How are your fighting skills, Rory?" he asked. "Elspeth said you fight well. Would you care to spar with me?" He nudged the pot with his boot. "This won't be ready for some time."

Rory glanced at me and Ignis. "Is this a trick?"

"Don't look at me," I told him.

'You have much to learn from one another,' was Ignis's contribution.

Altrys rose and picked up a fallen branch and snapped twigs from its length. He tossed it to Rory and found another, repeating the process.

"Sticks?" the Druid asked, holding his up. "Are you serious?"

"We have a long road ahead of us, Druid. The last thing either of us needs is an avoidable injury."

Rory snorted. "You hear that, Elspeth? He's dreamy *and* wise."

"*Dùin do ghob*," I drawled in Gaelic. "Entertain me, already."

The two men assumed their positions and began bickering amongst themselves, whacking each other with their practice sticks. They better work out their pacing order soon because I couldn't tolerate an entire week of this. Right now, I was worried about the prospect of meeting my mother more than the status of my relationships.

Looking to the darkening forest around the camp, I began to settle, the sounds of Altrys and Rory's sparring fading into the background.

My senses vibrated, picking up on the ebb and flow of magic in the earth beneath us. It was faint, but like all things Fae, even the dirt and rocks were permeated with power. Nature was more alive in the world than on Earth, hence the existence of the elementals.

Remembering the night the Chimera attacked us on the road to Sil Astrad, the words of the spirits of the forests echoed through my memories. *Ak'ande la. Save him…*

Looking to Altrys, I studied the strong angles in

his body and felt the spark of his muted magic as he fought Rory. This world wanted him to live, but why?

Perhaps it wasn't for us to know until it was time for the grand design to reveal itself. I knew how that felt.

'Altrys wants to know if Rory is full of shite,' Ignis declared suddenly.

I choked on my own spit, causing the men to falter and glance at me. Rory took the opening in his stride and whacked the *Shr'lei* on his sword arm with his stick.

'It's true,' the cat added. *'I'd do the same thing if I had opposable thumbs.'*

10

We continued our journey north, the days becoming colder as we approached An Valran.

The purplish smudge on the horizon gained form, etching into rugged mountains that stretched into the clouds. The air thinned as we went up in altitude, and frost hounded our little camps every evening.

I'd never missed the modern conveniences of cars, hotels, and central heating as much as I did right now. Part of me wanted to reach for my Colour—just a little spark to warm my fingertips—but the lingering threat of the Chimera stopped me.

The animosity between Rory and Altrys had seemed to settle after their training session with their sticks. It wasn't an unfortunate euphemism, either. They'd continued to duel every night after we'd made camp like they were chasing some arbitrary high score.

Me? Well, I listened to the currents of nature in an attempt to puzzle out the mysteries of the world that birthed the Fae and their ruthless ancestors, the Tuatha de Danann.

But the elementals were silent.

If they roamed these wild reaches, then they weren't interested in what we were doing.

However, magic wasn't the only thing I heard in the dark of night. Animals and unknown creatures roamed the lonely backroads, their scratching and foraging sending ripples through the earth.

We were two nights away from Lir Cael when a blood-curdling shriek echoed through the stillness of our wild camp.

I sat bolt upright, my heart beating wildly as the horses began to whicker and lay their ears back. Ignis rustled inside the blanket next to me—he liked being the little spoon—and poked his head out.

"What is that?" Rory whispered as he rose.

The fire had burned down to coals, a light breeze making them flare, but it gave no light—not enough to see anything by, anyway.

Altrys sat up next to me and pressed his finger to his lips, urging us to be still.

'*Something strays close*,' Ignis said, the only one able to talk.

We huddled in the darkness, listening. The normal sounds of the forest stilled—the rustling of foliage, the creak of branches, the foraging of animals—and the world become deathly silent.

At first there was nothing, then came a low groan and the magic in the earth vibrated, reaching out towards us.

Altrys held up his hand, warning us to remain still.

I drew in a shaking breath, my eyes straining to decipher the shadows. Then a creature rose from behind the rise above our camp and grew until its head nearly reached the treetops. It was pitch-black with long, twisted antlers that merged so seamlessly with the thick woods, I imagined it was a part of them, like an extension of the magic that flowed through this place.

But its outline was all that I could make out. It cast an ominous feeling over everything that saw it, including me.

The creature loomed, watching us for a long moment, it true shape hidden. Finally, it moved away from us, continuing along the rise. Its huge lumbering body moved out of sight and all was still.

It was some time before Altrys spoke. By then, the creature had passed beyond the valley and the forest had awoken once again.

"I did not expect to find one here," he said as the first signs of dawn began to lighten the sky through the canopy. "They never venture far from the forest's heart."

I shivered and pulled Ignis into my lap. "What was it? It had to be at least seven-feet-tall."

"A kai'ash," Altrys replied. "An ancient guardian of the forest."

'*A guardian?*' Ignis enquired. '*What does it guard?*'

"The forest," the Fae told him. "With single-minded purpose."

"Why did it just pass us like that?" I held Ignis close and the little cat squirmed in my grasp. "It looked right at us."

"We have no quarrel with it," Altrys explained. "We've taken only what we need to sustain our passing."

"And if we had taken more?" Rory asked.

The *Shr'lei* shrugged. "We'd already be dead."

"Well, that wasn't ominous at all," I drawled.

"It's gone now, but I still want to check the forest," Altrys said, rising. "Stay here. I won't be long."

He grabbed his sword and the bow off his horse, spiriting away into the forest before my frozen mind could formulate a response.

Rory looked at me, his brow creased.

"What?" I whispered.

"Our people have seen them before," he replied. "I've never seen them, of course, but…"

My expression fell and I understood. "They're the creatures that roam the Darklands."

He nodded. "It was a Relic."

My mind tumbled with an onslaught of new information. I tried to make sense of some of it, but it was like a puzzle with a million fragments… that only had half the pieces.

I swallowed hard. "What if the heart of the forest is…"

"It might be a place in space time where worlds cross," he murmured. "Another way into the Darklands."

I wanted it to be true. Rory wanted to find the homeland so badly, it had almost consumed him once already. If he chased that creature back to wherever it came from, it might just claim his life.

"Or it might just be a fragment left behind by the meddling of the Old Ones," I told him. "No one knows who they were or why they made the Darklands, Rory. Can you say with any certainty that they created those creatures? Merlin made a pact with them to protect the homeland. That nightmare world wasn't made for us. It was repurposed."

"Merlin?" He blinked and looked away. "What does he have to do with anything?"

"*Everything*. It was in my father's journal," I replied. "Dad said Delilah suspected Merlin had made a deal with the Old Ones to conceal Thríbhís Mhór, so when the Druids returned home from their millennia of wandering, nothing could follow them. But they had a price."

"The Darklands," he murmured, his complexion turning grey. "The souls of the unworthy."

"Our people were the price. The Relics—"

"You said she *suspected* it," he snapped.

"We don't have an entire world to ourselves. So what?" I hissed. "So we weren't good enough to join the other Druids in some utopia? *So what?* We have a home, each other, and a universe to explore. Isn't that enough?"

Rory's expression darkened. "Then what did my parents die for?"

"You," I told him. "They died for you, but—" My throat tightened, and I blinked away a barrage of unexpected tears. "But they died because of me. Don't forget why we came here. *Please*."

Movement in the tree line revealed Altrys returning from his scout and Rory jerked away. "How could I?"

I grasped his arm and pulled him close. Rory tensed, his power rippling.

"You don't want to go chasing it," I murmured. "Not now."

He lowered his gaze. "You're not the only one who has a score to settle with the Chimera, Lor'Odhweine."

Tearing out of my grip, he stalked across the camp, shoving past a confused Altrys.

"I was only gone a few minutes," the Fae drawled. "What is upsetting the Druid this time?"

I stared at Rory as he saddled his horse, my heart heavy.

"There are things about my people you don't know," I said. "The Druids have secrets that cannot be spoken."

He drew in a deep breath and looked towards the forest. "He's seen a kai'ash before." It was a statement, one I wasn't prepared to confirm nor deny. "Is it sacred? This… secret."

"Deeply," I replied. "It's not my right to talk about it. I'd barely learned what it was to be a Druid before learning about my reality." Besides, there were other fish in line to fry before anyone could dare think about the Darklands. A cataclysm that could ultimately wipe the Druids off the face of the universe trumped Relic hunting.

"I understand."

"Come on," I said. "We better get moving if we want to reach Lir Cael in time for the meeting."

"Elspeth?"

I turned.

Altrys nodded towards Rory. "Is that something we have to worry about?"

"No," I told him. "Rory feels things deeply, but he's not a liability. I trust him with my life."

The *Shr'lei* nodded once and began to clear up our camp.

Sighing, I tipped the last of the water in our pot over the dying embers of the campfire.

Once we were on our way, our little group became eerily silent despite the surrounding beauty in the wilderness.

The higher we ventured, the more the landscape changed. Hardier pines, spruces, and furs took over from the oaks and evergreens of the lowlands. The ground became rockier and the road thinned until it was nothing more than an overgrown track.

When Altrys told us we'd be taking the way that was less travelled, he failed to mention we'd be scrambling along glorified animal trails. Still, neither Rory nor I complained. We had our own problems to think about, and they both trumped a little discomfort in the backside region.

In the end, it was Ignis who broke the awkward silence between Rory and me.

'I feel like I never left my home,' he declared.

I looked down, seeing he'd poked his head out of his furry bag.

'If you don't think about the magic or all those other things we're fighting, it could be Earth,' he added. *'Don't you think?'*

I glanced at Rory.

"All my life I've been yearning for someplace else," he murmured. "You have to understand, Elspeth."

"I do," I told him. "I grew up not fitting in. I came to Edinburgh, found you and the Druids, and I never fit in there, either… until I worked for it."

"It's not that," he went on. "It's our blood. We've wandered for so long, it yearns for the world it came from. All these places might feel like they could be home, but they're not."

"What if the price of home turns out being an eternity of wandering the Darklands as a slave to the Old Ones?" I asked. "What then?"

He turned his gaze forwards. "Then that's how it was meant to be."

"*Deash,*" Altrys hissed. "Quiet."

Ahead, the *Shr'lei* reined in his horse and held up his hand. His gaze was fixed to the road ahead as Rory and I came to a stop a few feet behind him.

Something wasn't right. I felt it in the air as soon as silence fell over us. The hairs stood up on the back of my neck as I scanned the thick woods on either side of us, but nothing moved, save for the wind through the treetops.

I glanced at Rory as he reached for his sword.

'*We are not alone,*' Ignis said. '*A lonely road makes for easy profit.*'

'*Robbers?*' I wondered.

'*It's not Chimera.*'

"*Ah'ila!*" a rasping voice cried.

Movement erupted in the shadows of the forest as several men tossed their camouflaged cloaks away and burst out of the forest.

They were De'ashlide. Five armed, angry, dangerous De'ashlide men. We were so getting robbed right now.

An arrow flew past my head with a whoosh. My horse neighed in fright, tossing its head back, and stamped its hooves. I grasped for my sword, tearing it free from the scabbard as I tried to tighten my hold on the reins to keep the animal's head down.

Spotting the archer in a tree ahead to the left, I called out to Altrys, "Tree! Eleven o'clock!"

With one swift movement, the *Shr'lei* strung his bow and sent an arrow flying into the branches. A cry of pain rang out, then the sound of something large crashing through the canopy, then a thud as the body hit the ground.

It didn't stop the advance of the De'ashlide, their swords glinting as they brandished them at us.

A sixth figure dashed out of the forest and grabbed at my reins and I swore. Slashing at the attacker, I drove him back, but not before my hood slipped off my head.

"Unseelie!" the man shrieked. "Shri'danann *za'adei!*"

Ignis leapt from the bag, his prisms stretching as he flew through the air. As he landed, his form shattered and his tiger shape solidified.

The De'ashlide froze, their eyes widening as Ignis opened his jaws and paced towards the man who'd grabbed me, a low growl rumbling deep in his throat.

The Fae stumbled and fell into a ditch with a cry. Ignis loomed over him and placed a large paw on his chest, holding the terrified De'ashlide in place.

Altrys wheeled his horse around and held up his hands. "Ignis, *addrei.*"

The tiger retracted his claws, but never took his paw off the man.

Altrys spoke to the De'ashlide in Fae, the meaning of his words lost on me, but I managed to pick out a few that I knew—death, fight, and stop. He seemed to be making a good case.

Rory glanced at me, his hand tightening around the hilt of his sword, his expression saying everything. *If they fought us, they would die.*

The moment I knew things would go south, was when the leader reached for his knife.

Ignis didn't hesitate. He latched onto the De'ashlide, tearing at the man's throat.

"Leave the horses," Altrys cried as he leapt from his mount. He slapped it on the rump with the flat of his sword, and it took off into the forest with a terrified neigh.

Rory and I followed his lead, letting our faithful horses disappear after their leader. There were advantages to fighting on horseback, but on this trail, it was a death trap.

We fought side by side, parrying blows and pushing our attackers back. Ignis leapt on a Fae a moment before he landed a blow on Rory, dragging him down and tearing him open with his claws.

The death of each Fae stabbed at me like white-hot pokers, their abrupt passing almost threatened to drag me through the veil with them. The sensation was stronger than I'd ever felt, more than it had when we'd been ambushed on the road from Un Alari.

My power was growing, which could only mean the prophecy was catching up with me, and *fast.*

There was no time to think about it now.

I spun and ducked as a sword slashed towards me. Thrusting my blade, I caught my attacker in the side, the steel tearing through flesh. Remembering Altrys's lessons, I used the momentum of my body and twisted around, driving my sword backwards and up.

It hit flesh and bone, sinking into the De'ashlide with horrifying ease. The moment the tip of my blade pierced his heart, my entire body shuddered as the veil snatched his soul and tore it into the surging currents of death.

I pulled my sword free and rose, stepping to the side as the body fell lifelessly to the ground.

"Are you all right?" Altrys asked, his chest heaving.

'They were all dead.'

"Elspeth?"

I nodded and turned as I caught the sound of footsteps hurrying down the road behind us.

One last De'ashlide thief fled, his fear guiding his flight. His arms flailed as he glanced over his shoulder at us.

"He has seen us now," Altrys said. "We can't let him go."

I shook my head. "I could trap him like I did to Mindel. Come back for him later."

"We can't use magic," Rory told me, his expression troubled. "I wouldn't risk it."

"There will be others." Altrys strung an arrow in his bow and drew the string back. He held it steady, tracking the fleeing De'ashlide… then he let the arrow loose.

It flew with surprising speed, the fletchings twirling hypnotically. I closed my eyes a moment before it hit, but it didn't stop me feeling the moment the man's life ended. The veil shuddered, then welcomed his soul with a satisfied sigh.

"Are you all right?" Rory asked.

"It was easy to block it out in the city. Death is a normal part of life, but killing?" I shook my head as Altrys stood before us.

"I'm sorry, Elspeth," he murmured. "These De'ashlide were criminals. Even if we weren't… It is my duty to hand them justice because they attacked us."

"And if they hadn't?" Rory asked.

"They would be judged by the Lor'andann."

The Druid sighed and looked down at the blood on his sword. I knew he would stew over what had just happened for weeks. Even though Rory had grown up fighting the Chimera, killing didn't come easy. The Druids were supposed to be pacifists, not warriors.

"Is it that easy?" he asked the *Shr'lei*. "Don't you care?"

"I do not find it rewarding, Druid," Altrys replied with a scowl. "I never want to kill another Fae, especially not a De'ashlide, but I have to in this world." He glanced at the man lying on the road. "And so do they."

'This is not how he wants equality in his world to be won,' Ignis said to me.

'No one does,' I replied. *'Least of all their alleged goddess of death.'*

"I don't like it either, but they wouldn't have asked

us to hand over our valuables," I told Rory. "He tried."

"Come," Altrys said, his shoulders tense. "Let's find our horses." He walked towards the man lying on the road. "They won't have gone far."

11

———

'*It bothers him*,' Ignis said the next morning.

'*Who?*' I asked as I readied my horse for the final ascent into Lir Cael.

It had been a restless night lingering in the woods without a fire to warm us, so we all felt a little worse for wear. Yesterday's events weighed heavily on all of us in different ways.

'*Altrys*,' the cat replied. '*Having to kill those Fae when he is one of them.*'

I glanced at the *Shr'lei*, wondering when we'd begun to drift apart. Since leaving Sil Astrad, the air had thickened between us and our easy way together seemed more difficult. I regretted that it'd taken me so long to realise.

It was something more than Rory's jealousy, even though he seemed to have let that go since the attack yesterday. A silent mark of respect had bloomed between the men, but they were still far from besties.

Lir Cael loomed and so did my prophecy. It put us all on edge.

And at midnight tonight, I might meet my mother.

'We all do things we don't like,' I told Ignis. *'I've killed Chimera. I still think about Mindel and his followers that I trapped in death. They're still there…'*

Ignis didn't reply as I mounted my horse, falling in behind Altrys as we left our camp behind. Rory brought up the rear, his Colour simmering. I wasn't the only one on edge.

By mid-afternoon, we found the main road.

Glancing up both ways, I tugged at my hood to make sure it wouldn't fall. We were alone for now, but this part of the world was sparsely populated, and the hour didn't bode well for travellers. It was a lesson we'd learned the hard way.

We wove between rocky outcrops and boulders the size of houses, passing in and out of the long shadows cast by the setting sun. The cloud-streaked sky burned orange and purple, the light playing over the mountains, turning them into a landscape painting.

Despite the beauty, I squirmed in my saddle. Every hoofbeat made my anxiety rise more than it ever had. I had avoided thinking about what we might find waiting for us tonight, but now I had to acknowledge it.

I'd finally become used to being the *Liash li Ashli,* and now my life was about to change yet again.

As the first stars began to appear in the sky above, Lir Cael finally emerged between the crags. Lights blinked through the dense woodland that hugged the edge of the mountain range as the final rays of the sun struck the highest peak far within the wilderness, igniting the snowcapped summit like a flaming torch.

"What do people do here?" Rory asked as we continued along the road.

"They mine," Altrys replied, "gold, silver, copper, and stone. There are three major mines and a quarry."

"What about the landslides?" I wondered. "I thought Lir Cael had been buried before?"

"The original city lies farther into An Valran. It's still buried, along with a great deal of old mines and those who worked them. There are some ruins, but no one goes there."

"They probably think they're haunted," Rory said. "I wouldn't be surprised if they were."

I shivered, more from the thought of so many people trapped under the mountain that had given them opportunity and life… only for it to become their tomb. Just to be on the safe side, I clamped my mind around my senses, dulling them to the veil and the things that reached for it.

As we entered the outer edges of the village, I craned my neck, curious as to what it looked like. Altrys had told us all about it and I'd imagined an ancient elaborate city made of carved stone, but the real thing was way simpler, but no less interesting.

Steep paths carved into the rock face led up to buildings that had been constructed on every available patch of earth. Each house had a roof of mottled slate and dappled quartz, the walls made of quarried rock. The eaves, windowsills, and doors were ornately carved wood featuring the animals of the forest and mountains entwined with the trees and flowers of the region.

It reminded me of a mixture between an old Norse village and something out of a fantasy tale. I imagined dwarves and gnomes tunnelling into the mountain in search of precious stones, but in fact, the reality was just as fantastical. Once I'd been a simple human being in a world without magic, and now I was in the world of the Fae where magic ran parallel to everything, even the De'ashlide.

We kept to the outskirts, taking a wide berth around the centre of the village where the Lor'andann's residence lay. Much like Un Alari, most of the people here were De'ashlide. I could tell they worked in the mines from the way they moved to the clothes they wore. It was one of the only jobs to be had around here, other than the other traditional workings of the town.

We stabled our horses at the tavern, taking our few belongings with us. I waited outside with Rory and Ignis—who still huddled in his bag—while Altrys went inside to arrange a room for us in the inn upstairs.

Leaning in the shadows, I scanned the quiet street.

The cold had driven everyone indoors in search of warmth, but a few stragglers hurried here and there. Quartz-topped light posts glowed bright with magical fire, lighting the cobbled road and reflecting off the ice crystals in the air.

A banner hung from a building across the way. A hammer and anvil on a field of green, bordered with copper. Lir Cael was a city built—and rebuilt—on mines and forges, so it was no surprise they made their tools their official emblem.

"They call it a village, but it's more like a city," Rory murmured. "Did you see the windows in the cliff? There has to be a whole tunnel system within the mountain."

"Given their history with landslides," I mused, "I don't know if that's wise or clever."

'They will have a way to dig themselves out,' Ignis piped up. *'There's only so much bad luck people can take.'*

The tavern door opened and Altrys stuck his head out. Beckoning us inside, he told us he'd arranged a room upstairs. We trudged after him, the cold having seeped into our toes despite the fancy socks La'luin had made us promise to wear.

The room was simple but suited our needs... almost.

There were two beds, a fireplace, and a table and chairs. A modest tapestry hung on one wall, a chest sat in the far corner, and heavy, moss-green curtains hung over the window.

Ignoring the sleeping arrangements, I dumped my

bag against the wall. I unbuckled my sword and set it on the table, rolling my stiff shoulders. I was fitter than I'd ever been, but two restless nights and one sword battle later, I was a little rough around the edges.

Rory knelt before the fire and shoved logs into the hearth as Ignis wriggled out of his bag and shook his prisms out until he was the size of a house cat. He promptly began exploring every inch of the little room, sniffing in corners and climbing up onto the mantle.

"Stay here," Altrys told us. "I'm going to make some enquiries."

I nodded, shoving my hood back as Rory struck a flint, the spark catching on the tinder in the fireplace.

The Druid made a face as soon as the door closed. "Like we can't do anything ourselves."

"He knows the language," I told him, "and the customs. We'd out ourselves the moment we opened our mouths. We need this meeting to go smooth. I'm too tired and anxious for another ambush."

Rory sighed and sat on the bed. "Are you nervous?"

"You're asking me now?" I snorted, settling into a chair by the fire. "Of course, I am. I've wanted to know my mother my entire life, but now that I might get the chance… I'm…" I looked up at him. "I'm afraid of who she might be. She's a de Leiran and their reputation proceeds them, even though they're all dead."

"So are you and you're not an evil Unseelie necromancer hell-bent on destruction."

I narrowed my eyes. "Yet."

"Don't forget you're also an Odhweine. You use your Druid abilities far more than your Fae. It might be what saves you in the end."

I sighed as my stomach resumed its churning. Like I needed the reminder.

Ignis leapt off the mantle and prowled across the table. 'You've faced worse.'

I grunted and held my hands out towards the fire. "What did the message say again?"

"I never saw the whole thing," Rory admitted. "But there wasn't much on it to begin with. A time, a place, and a name. Aurae de Leiran." He played absently with the hem of his cloak. "It's a pretty name, don't you think? Aurae, like Aurora Borealis."

"Well, I guess we're in the right place for the Northern Lights."

"I studied a lot of maps while you travelled from Un Alari," Rory told me. "The landmasses are all different from Earth, but right now… I guess we're in what might be considered northern Finland or Norway. If we were in our own world, that is."

I noted that he'd said 'our world'. The Relic sighting had inflamed old wounds in him, but deep down, he saw Edinburgh and the Warren as home. His search for the homeland was something deeper, something magical in his blood, perhaps.

"Then where does the portal go? Sil Astrad can't be in Ireland. It's too far."

"It's difficult to say. The distances and weather patterns are out of alignment. A season lasts an entire year, for starters. This planet evolved so differently than Earth."

He could say that again. "This world makes no sense—"

A knock at the door startled me and I placed a hand over my heart.

Rory opened the door. Seeing Altrys through the crack, the Druid let him in.

The Fae carried a tray laden with three bowls of steaming food, complete with bread and cheese on the side. A garland hung around his wrist as he balanced the load, sliding the food onto the table as I moved my sword out of the way.

"The lor'ashlar lay on the west side of the village in the forest," Altrys stated. "It's a beautiful and secluded spot, or so I'm told."

"What are the flowers for?" I ran my fingers over the pine and berry laden sprigs that'd been twisted into a tight, little circle. A few white flowers had been tied into the arrangement, too. It was quite pretty.

"I told the maid I had dead I wished to pay my respects to," he replied. "She gave them to me to take as offerings."

"Really?" I asked. "You have family here?"

Altrys smirked and shook his head. "No. I needed reason to ask after the lor'ashlar that wouldn't raise suspicion. They don't easily trust outsiders here, travellers less. *Shr'lei?* Not at all."

"No one would want to come here to sightsee, that's for sure," Rory muttered, poking at his food. When he'd decided it was adequate, he began shovelling it into his mouth.

Altrys broke some bread and offered me some.

I shook my head, my stomach too unsettled to even think about food. "Later… I should go in on my own."

Rory coughed. "I don't think——"

"It's me she wants to speak to. If I bring along a Druid, a *Shr'lei*, and a prismatic cat, it will spook her. If it's not my mother, then you'll be taken or worse. I have the power to escape, if not…" I glanced at Altrys.

He swallowed hard and looked away, busying himself with his dinner.

"No," Rory said firmly. "Ignis should stay with you. If things turn bad, he can protect you until Altrys and I can arrive. He can fit in your pocket."

"But——"

"No buts," he interrupted. "I know you don't need protecting, Elspeth, but I also know you don't want to use your powers if you don't have to. We can help you."

"Using your magic will also give you away to the Chimera," Altrys added, his tone turning formal. "The aim will be to neutralise any ambush before they can get word of your presence to their leaders. Your identity and location must remain secret at all costs. If this meeting gleans information that will help us strike at their heart, we must retain the element of surprise at all costs."

I scowled, surprised at the anger rising in my veins. The veil brushed against my fingers unbidden and I shoved my hands underneath my cloak.

"So, you've worked it all out, then," I muttered sourly.

Altrys said nothing, his silence striking me where it hurt—directly in the heart.

'It is a wise plan,' Ignis said. *'You are more than a prophecy, Elspeth. Your life means more than that.'*

Reaching out, I scratched him under the chin. *'That's what I wanted him to say.'*

Ignis lifted his head. 'Perhaps you should say it so he can hear.'

'It hurts, but I don't want to make it harder on him. If he has to... I don't want to hurt him more than I will already.'

'Rory is wise,' the cat told me. *'You should listen to him.'*

'About what?'

'You are your father's daughter.'

"They're having a silent conversation again," Rory said with a sigh. "I almost want to curse La'luin for giving the fleabag his voice back."

"You're not missing out on much," I told them.

"We have four hours," Altrys murmured. "We should use it wisely."

"Elspeth, you should eat first," Rory said, pushing a bowl towards me. "It will settle your stomach."

I picked up a spoon. "Thanks."

Ignis stared at Altrys, his eyes narrowing. *'Is some of that for me?'*

"I thought you didn't need food," the Fae replied.

'I don't… but that doesn't mean I don't like to eat.'

12

The cemetery—the *Ashlar an lor*—was nestled in a secluded pocket of woodland outside of Lir Cael.

Darkness clung almost absolute, the trees towering so tall, I imagined their pointed tops brushed against the clouds. Somewhere out there, Altrys and Rory hid, waiting to see who would greet me amongst the *lor'ashlar*.

I breathed deeply, my lungs filling with chilled air. The forest smelt like pine, with the faint tang of metal from the smelting works at the mines that lay farther into the mountain range.

Ignis slunk through the shadows in his tabby cat shape, weaving around the *lor'ashlar* like a ghost. I checked my hood, burying into it for warmth and safety.

On any other night, the sight of the hundreds of stone shrines would have been beautiful. Back in Un

Alari, Altrys had told me the Fae respected the dead above most things. Paying respects to the descaled was expected as a mark of honour.

The Fae's burial rites were heavily linked to the elements of life. Bodies were cleansed by fire to return to the air. The ashes were buried at the base of a *lor'ashlar* to return to the earth. Once their souls were free of their mortal bindings, their spirits climbed, gathering the wisdom of life's endeavours before they ventured into the next life.

The carvings twisting up each totem represented deeds done by the dead. The more important someone was, the taller their shrine. Each held at least one hollow inside the stone where offerings could be placed. Many held candles that glowed as I passed, their families tending to them daily. Everywhere I looked, tiny points of light glowed as if the woods were alive with fireflies.

Fireflies of the dead, I thought morosely.

'An eerie beauty in the place of the departed,' Ignis agreed, mistaking my observation as speech.

'Can you sense anyone?'

It was a moment before the cat replied. *'Yes and no...'*

'Illusion?' I wondered.

'Perhaps.'

I kept to the shadows, listening for the approach of my unknown appointment. The night stretched through the *Ashlar an lor*, my eyes squinting as every shrine became the embodiment of a person or an imaginary Chimera army.

My skin prickled, every hair on my body standing on end. Plumes of white vapour billowed before me as I let my breath out, my nerves completely shot.

Where was she?

I wished I had a watch to check, wondering why everyone on this planet happened to just know what time it was. I hadn't seen a watch, clock, or anything. How they knew without ever having to look at the sun or the stars was beyond me.

Ignis lurked just out of sight, prowling around the *lor'ashlar*. That's when I saw a figure standing in the dim light cast by several candles inside a tall shrine. The top was carved into the shape of an eagle with its wings spread in flight—a strong, glorious creature—but I wasn't interested, not at that moment.

The hooded figure was so still I wondered if they were another statue. I waited, staring at their back and willing them to move.

From their slight build, I guessed it was a woman. My heart leapt and I broke out in a cold sweat. *Was it her?*

Letting go of my senses, they flowed across the *Ashlar an lor* and brushed up against unknown magic. She was Shri'danann at least, but that didn't comfort me. Magic was beautiful, but it was also deadly.

If I wanted to know if the woman was my mother or an elaborate trap, then I'd have to make the first move. She was waiting for me, after all.

My heart beat wild as I stepped out of the shadows. I stared at the woman's back, my boots treading softly on the trail, ready to strike if I had to. My fingers brushed over the hilt of my knife, finding little comfort in the fact I was being watched by Rory and Altrys. I'd become a warrior, one who could handle anything on her own.

The veil surged forwards, responding to my emotions, and I shoved it back. *Not yet.*

"Who are you?" I murmured, my voice full with an unspoken warning.

The woman turned, unsurprised at my sudden appearance. Her eyes flashed silver under her hood, but her features remained in shadow.

"You came."

The sound of her voice slammed into me and my hand fell away from my knife. My anger melted away, my expression falling with it.

"Who are you?" I asked again. "*Identify yourself.*"

The woman lifted her hands and pulled her hood back, revealing emerald green hair. *Unseelie.*

My heart almost stopped beating.

She was older than I was, perhaps in her forties or fifties, but there were no wrinkles to denote age—that was all in her eyes. Wisdom, knowing, and power radiated in her silver eyes with stunning familiarity.

"I am Aurae de Leiran," she murmured, holding out her hands. "I come unarmed... *daughter.*"

I jerked my hood back, my throat tightening. Her gaze moved to my hair.

"It is you." Her lips curved into a smile. "You have your father's eyes… and his grandmother's name. Elspeth."

I said nothing. Honestly, I wasn't sure what reaction I'd have when I saw her. Anger wasn't one I thought I'd have to deal with, and it was currently growing again.

"I never thought I'd ever see you again. When I heard you had returned, I…" Aurae took a deep breath, tears misting her eyes. "I knew it was dangerous, but I had to warn you."

"I know," I told her thinly. "I know about it all."

"What of your father?" she asked, looking around the *Ashlar an lor*. "Where is Gordan?"

"Dead."

Her breath caught and she shook her head. "How?"

My lip curled. "The Chimera finally caught up with us."

Aurae choked back a sob and held out her hands towards me. I pulled back and she recoiled as if I'd slapped her.

It wasn't the reaction I'd envisioned, but I didn't know her. *At all.* My entire life, I'd wrapped myself in the thought of who and what she might be, not giving much thought to the reality of her identity. Aurae de Leiran was a stranger who owed me one hell of an explanation.

"I want to know what happened," I demanded. "*All of it.*"

"Not here," she murmured. "There are eyes everywhere. I have risked much by revealing myself. We cannot linger."

I regarded her for a moment, attempting to judge her sincerity. There was no doubt she was my mother, but her story was another matter.

Finally, I lifted my hand. Movement rustled across the fallen pine needles to my left and Altrys ghosted out of the shadows with his bow in his hands, an arrow notched and ready to fly. Ignis joined him, scurrying to my side, and Rory appeared from the right, his knife at the ready.

Aurae didn't seem surprised, though when she laid eyes on Ignis, her expression changed. Her gaze flew to Rory and back to me.

"The Druids came?" she whispered.

"What you did drove them to war," I hissed.

"You don't understand, he cannot be here. The Chim—"

"We know more than you think we do," I interrupted. "And now I want to know what you want with me, *Mother*. You owe me."

"Of course." She looked at Altrys.

"I am Altrys, *Shr'lei de Delei'an*," he told her. "I come on the queen's authority."

"Raurich Maerinn," Rory stated, pushing in. "Ambassador for the Druids. I speak on behalf of my people."

Aurae nodded, her silver eyes flickering to me. She

wanted to know my allegiance, but I wasn't willing to show my hand until she explained herself.

"I know a place that is neutral," she said after a moment. "It is safe."

"And if you betray us, know we will kill you without hesitation," the *Shr'lei* said.

"I would not expect anything less. We live in troubled times."

"Get on with it," I told her.

Aurae nodded once. "This way."

We followed her at a distance as the *Ashlar an lor* began to thin. We reached what seemed like a dead end, but my mother continued through the rocks. A hidden path cut into the cliff, the uneven steps disappearing amongst the crags above.

"Can we trust her?" Rory whispered, looking up at the steep trail.

I shrugged, watching Altrys follow Aurae up the stairs. "Right now, we have to."

"You don't seem happy."

I glanced at him. "That woman is a stranger to me. I didn't expect…"

"Don't worry," he told me. "You'll get your chance to know the truth of who she is, Chimera or no Chimera."

He began to climb, leaving me and Ignis at the bottom of the stairs. I looked up at the sky and sighed. Finally, we followed.

There was nowhere else to go.

Aurae took us through the wilderness and up the mountain.

Hidden from the outside world, nestled between a ridge and a cliff, hidden by trees and rock, lay a cave where she had made her home.

It was nothing much to look at. The furniture was simple, made from hardy wood and stone. A table sat beside a small kitchen area, while two armchairs hugged a modest fireplace. In the far corner was a bed with a large chest at its foot.

How the mighty de Leirans had fallen.

I made myself at home, not waiting for an invitation. I sat beside the fire and Ignis leapt into my lap, taking a protective stance, his green eyes following Aurae's every movement.

"When you're ready," I declared, raising my eyebrows. *This ought to be good.*

'*I'm curious, too,*' Ignis commented.

Aurae glanced at Altrys and Rory.

"Anything you have to say to me, they can hear it," I told her. "I trust them with my life and they with mine."

"Very well." She gestured to the room. "My home is yours."

Altrys positioned himself by the door, leaning against the wall with his sword drawn. Rory took the edge of the bed, his gaze hard.

"I met Gordan in the last days of the war," Aurae

began, settling into the other chair for the long haul. "When it was clear to my father that the Unseelie clans would lose, he had us move to our family residence in these very mountains. It stands beside the Pale Lake, Il Fir, but it is long abandoned. The de Leirans were feared, as you have likely been told." Aurae sighed and turned her face towards the fire. "They deserved it."

"And you?" I asked, narrowing my eyes.

"I was hidden my entire life," she replied. "There were hopes that I would be born with the power of death, but if it was known a daughter had been born to our family… I was hidden for my safety. I knew nothing else. Was I good? Perhaps."

"But you didn't manifest any powers," I murmured. "Did you?"

She shook her head. "No. I never did, but it wouldn't matter to our enemies. They would cut me down where I stood if they knew I even existed."

There was that annoying fear thing again. The Seelie would rather drive a sword through her heart than wait to see if she held the power of the veil as I did. During war, Aurae would have been used as a weapon to win it for the Unseelie, and ultimately, eradicate the rule and existence of the Tuatha and Celestine royal line. The world would have been an entirely different place.

"It was a lonely life," she went on. "As a child, my only friends were servants who were too afraid of what I might be to not humour the longings of a lonely girl. When we moved to Il Fir, I was a young woman who understood the reality of my imprisonment and the truth of who my father was. All I wanted was to be free." Her expression twisted and she dabbed at her eyes. "I wanted to see the world outside. To breathe the air, to walk the forest, to skate across the frozen Pale Lake, to speak to someone. *Anyone.*"

"What of your mother? Your other family?" I asked.

"They were all killed. Our family was hunted down and slaughtered. My mother—your grandmother—was taken when I was four years old. I remained in our ancestral home until I was twenty, then I was at Il Fir for five years."

"You were alone all that time?" Rory asked.

"Yes… until I could bear it no more and escaped. I only intended to visit the lake for an evening and return. There was nowhere else for me to go. No city, no village, nothing."

"How do you meet my father?" I asked.

"I remember being in the forest when the portal opened that night. It was winter, snow lay thick on the ground, and my toes had become numb despite my boots. A man appeared. He was tall, wore strange clothing, and his magic… It was like nothing I'd ever felt before. Like… crystals." Rory glanced at me as Aurae continued, lost in her memory of my dad, "At first, I was wary of him, but something inside my heart told me he meant no harm. From there he came back almost every night. He told me about his home, and I told him about mine. I knew his power would be coveted if anyone discovered him, and if they discovered my absences... But we were in love. The risk was worth it for those stolen moments." Aurae closed her eyes and smiled, a tear rolling down her cheeks. "That year was the happiest of my entire life. He loved me for who I was, not what I could become."

"Would he love you for who you are now?" I asked.

"Elspeth," Rory hissed.

Aurae glanced at him. "It is an honest question, Druid."

"And?" I prodded.

"I don't know," she replied. "I'm not the same person I was then. I've done things to stay alive, hoping that one day I would get to see you again while praying you would stay far, far away."

I nodded. It was a fair answer. "What happened next? How did the Chimera discover you?"

"The Chimera..." She sighed. "My father had aligned himself with those fanatics during the war. They wanted the same things—to dominate—and both believed they were manipulating the other."

It was also a tinderbox waiting to ignite and engulf them all in uncontrollable fire.

"When I found out I was with child, I knew I couldn't keep the truth from my father... or the Chimera," she continued. "It was only matter of time, but I still tried. When my father learned about my pregnancy, he had me locked away and ordered Gordan found before the fanatics could find him." She shook her head. "*I was so naïve.*"

I snorted. "You were."

"He would have taken you and turned you into a monster, Elspeth. The Chimera would have done worse. And if the Seelie had learned of your impending birth, they would have marched on Il Fir and burned it to the ground with us inside. We couldn't let that happen. The only place you would be safe was in Gordan's world with his people."

"Yeah, right." I scowled and stroked my hand along Ignis's back. It hadn't worked out that way... far from it.

Aurae stared at me, confused. She glanced at Rory and Altrys, silently begging for someone to explain.

"You tell her, Rory," I muttered. "I don't have the strength."

So that's what he did, and he left nothing out. War, fear, and death had been the only things that had followed me and my dad through the portal to Earth. That, and a lifetime of running.

"I never knew," I murmured. "About you, about this world, about any of it."

"You are precious, Elspeth. It was all to save you from the suffering I endured."

"You were playing with fire the night you met my dad and you knew it," I hissed. "And you dared to drag him into it anyway. You were selfish, Aurae. *Selfish.*"

"I loved him," she cried. "He's gone, but… *I will always love him.*"

I rose to my feet, almost sending Ignis flying. "If you loved him, you would have let him go long before you created me."

"I never planned for this to happen, daughter. You have to understand that everything I did, I did for you as a mother should, and I am your mother still. I will always love Gordan, and I will always love you. I am so sorry." She fell to her knees and clasped her hands together. "*Ahleida da, anahlei. Ahleida da… ahleida da.*"

It's pathetic, isn't it? the voice inside my head remarked. *The powerful Aurae de Leiran on her knees, sobbing like a child.*

I understood now. Yenris'del was Aurae's servant who plotted with her and my father to smuggle me out of Il Fir and through a portal to the Warren, but it was already too late. The Chimera had followed, and the rest was history.

Now I was here, not far from where I was born, with the Chimera still searching for their child of prophecy. No one had saved anyone and now it was up to me to fix their bullshit mistakes.

"*Get up,*" I snapped. "You didn't send that message so you could cry for forgiveness at my feet. You have information about the Chimera, don't you?"

She wiped her eyes and hung her head. "I know

where their stronghold is," she murmured. "I know how we can end them once and for all."

Altrys looked at me, his eyes widening. I grimaced, knowing what he'd say—*be careful, the Chimera are cunning,* or something like it. Rory, on the other hand, was practically frothing at the mouth.

"Then you better start talking," I told my mother. "Because it might be the only thing that redeems you after what you've done."

13

———

Aurae told us everything she knew as the night stretched into the dawn.

After my father and I returned to Earth, the civil war ended, my grandfather was executed, and my mother went into hiding. She never existed to the outside world, so it wasn't difficult for her to disappear. All she had to do was outsmart the Chimera.

In the twenty-five years since, she'd lived on the fringes of society, waiting and hoping for a chance to put a stop to the Chimera. The prophecy had brought me back before she could find a solution, but she knew the location of their stronghold, their numbers, and the identity of their leader... and here we were.

Aurae told us she'd found the Chimera stronghold in the frozen wilds of An Valran, in the shadow of its tallest peak, Si Ithqua—loosely translated as the Mountain of Glass—named for its vast glaciers. It seemed the perfect place to hide; desolate and inaccessible to all but the hardiest mountaineers. Even those with magic struggled to climb into the wilderness.

A thousand disciples followed the twisted doomsday religion, their number stretching across the Fae realm. Agents had buried themselves into every part of the Fae culture, government, and military… just like Larel had in Un Alari. Even now, the gears of manipulation were turning in preparation for my return.

We'd stopped nothing, merely delayed the inevitable. War was coming, with or without me, but it wasn't the war I was used to seeing. On Earth, war was guns, tanks, and airstrikes; it was trenches and explosions, fronts and machine-gun posts.

In this world, war began with subterfuge and lies. The killing with magic and swords came later, only when the true pillars of power—the royal family and the Lor'andann's—were toppled.

When Altrys questioned Aurae, she told us about her abilities and how they allowed her to sneak inside without their knowing.

My mother's magic was similar to mine, though she didn't have the curse that helped me manipulate the veil. She could phase, which explained how I could when it didn't seem to correlate with anything else I could do, and had an infinity for illusions. It seemed I was a de Leiran in more ways than one… not that I wanted to be.

My Colour added another layer of complications. All the things I could do as a Fae were amplified and complimented by Druidic nature. Portals, illusions, and the prisms that grew out of the very fabric of nature itself. As a Spirit Walker, the black sun burned darker than ever.

But I already knew about that with painful clarity.

When Aurae had told us everything she knew, I turned and left the cave, emerging into the dull morning, the name she had spoken weighing heavy in my mind. The name of the Chimera leader.

Vulis.

The door opened with a creak and closed with a thud. Rory stood beside me, Ignis lying around his neck like a scarf.

He sighed, his breath vaporising on the icy air. "What a mindf—"

"I don't want to talk about her."

"We have to talk about it eventually," he murmured.

I couldn't meet his gaze. "We're here for the Chimera."

Rory said nothing, neither did Ignis.

The door opened again, and this time Altrys appeared.

"Where's Aurae?" I asked.

He nodded towards the cave. "Inside. We will be departing without her... for now."

Leave her there, the voice said, the sound of it tugging at the veil. *Let her rot, rot, rot.*

"I think it's best we go back to the inn," the *Shr'lei* murmured. "The wind carries more than ice."

I nodded as I shoved away the veil, along with the voice that lured me closer to death. "Let's go then. I don't want to stay any longer than I have to."

We returned in silence to our room in the inn on the outskirts of Lir Cael as the sun finished its final ascent over the mountains.

There was nothing to say after the massive info-dump Aurae had tipped over my unsuspecting head. I needed time, but the longer we were in An Valran, the angrier I became.

"We are in a precarious position," Altrys mused, throwing another log onto the fire. Sparks flew up the chimney and warmth began to slowly spread into our room.

"How?" Rory asked.

"We have an opportunity to surprise them," he replied. "But their numbers give me pause. We need assistance from the *Shr'lei de Delei'an*, but we would lose any advantage by returning to the capital. Any force moving into Lir Cael would be seen… and met in kind."

Rory's brow furrowed and he turned to me. "Elspeth, you've seen the capital, could you phase?"

I shook my head. "I could probably go back, but returning with an army? I don't think even I could manage more than three or four in one day. We'd need a whole battalion to get into a place that size."

"That is if they could get there through the mountains," Altrys told us. "The weather is turning and An Valran is treacherous, even in summer."

"*Pfft,*" Rory spat. "Why is the perfect place for an evil lair always in the most irritating of places?"

'Are you really asking that?' Ignis asked with a yawn. *'A secret lair is exactly that. A secret.'*

"We have one chance," Altrys murmured. "If we lose the element of surprise, then it will escalate into outright war."

"If we kill this Vulis guy, someone else will just replace him," I argued. "Then someone else will replace the replacement. It's just a never-ending circle. To stop the Chimera, they all have to go."

Rory tensed and shook his head. "That would mean the prophecy…"

"If I did the killing, maybe," I said, narrowing my eyes. "But it's *all* Fae or *all* Druids. It's not targeted to one fanatical group or another."

"You must not use your magic, Elspeth," Altrys said, "under any circumstances."

I snorted. "I know that."

"Then what do you propose we do?" Rory asked. "The four of us sneak into the Chimera's fancy ice palace and murder a thousand fanatics in their sleep?"

The longer we argued about it, the more I realised there was no way to stop the coming cataclysm without it ending in another war. The Fae had barely begun to prosper in the wake of the last one. Could they stand together against the end of the world? I wanted to say yes, but the divisions I'd seen amongst the Shri'danann and De'ashlide were too great. Even the Seelie and Unseelie still harboured hatred for one another.

What kind of world had I pledged to save? Earth wasn't any better, yet I'd fought for it. Was it really about hope? Right now, it seemed like such a fickle concept.

Perhaps it was simply time to go for broke. Elspeth Odhweine's last stand. Let the black sun rise and take out the Chimera, and Altrys could end me before I lost control.

I glanced at him and my heart twisted. I'd opened myself to him, opened the places I'd locked long ago, hoping he… What was the point? Love was pointless for someone like me, who had the power to usher in a mass extinction with the click of her fingers.

Altrys's gaze met mine and I saw understanding there.

I sucked in a sharp breath and turned back to the fire, rather than acknowledge it.

"I'm going to scout the village," Altrys said after a moment. "We have a day or two at most to decide."

He left without waiting for a response, leaving Rory and I alone in the warmth of our little room. Ignis stretched, reaching his paws out as far as he could.

"I take it his silence means we're going to sneak into a creepy ice palace," Rory drawled.

"I don't like the snow," I admitted.

"Me, either."

Silence fell between us, the sounds of Lir Cael echoing through the walls. A shout, a slamming door, murmurings from the bar downstairs, the neigh of a horse, the rumble of carts climbing the steep roads towards the mines. My senses stirred, following the tunnels dug into the mountain by centuries of miners searching for the rich veins of ore threading through the rock.

The fire cracked and popped, making me blink.

"How are you really?" Rory asked. "You always wanted to meet your mother, but you seem…"

"I'm fine," I told him, my temples throbbing.

"You seem angry."

My fingers tightened around the hem of my cloak. The image of Aurae begging on her knees before me was a humiliating sight and yes, it made me angry. She hadn't even asked how Dad had died.

'Maybe she couldn't bear knowing,' Ignis purred.

'Get out of my head,' I snapped.

The cat flicked his tail and curled up on the bed. *'Then don't think so loud.'*

"I am angry," I admitted. "I expected more."

His eyebrows rose. "More what?"

I shrugged. "Love."

"She loved your father, Elspeth," Rory said with a

frown. "Love makes everyone go a little mad. I should know."

"Please don't make this about us," I whispered.

'He means well,' Ignis told me, but I ignored him.

"I don't think she intended for any of this to happen," Rory went on, "just like your father didn't. Bringing you to our world might have turned out badly, but it was the right thing to do. She gave up being your mother to save you from the same abuse she suffered."

It was startling coming from Rory, who'd lost his parents because of all this. Turning, I stared him. "You forgive her? After all the Chimera have done?"

"It was her father's doing," he told me. "The night she met your father, Aurae was the sum of all her experiences… her isolation and naivety drove her to make a drastic decision. She made a mistake the night she escaped Il Fir, but you were born out of love. I don't believe Gordan would have trusted her any other way. Druids don't let their feelings be known so easily."

"What about now?" I wondered. "Maybe her intentions have changed over the last twenty-five years."

"If she was telling the truth about her love, then she would never change. Unless it was for revenge, I suppose."

I snorted. "Who doesn't want revenge on the Chimera." But would she use her own daughter exact it? Aurae was a stranger to me, and she was Unseelie.

Whatever we did, we had to be careful. "Wait… She said no one knew of her because her father kept her hidden, yet Niarisshia knew her. She was the one who told me Aurae's name when I first arrived in Sil Astrad. Something doesn't add up."

"Twenty-five years is a long time," Rory mused.

"I don't think anyone would ever forget meeting someone like Niarisshia. Do you?"

His frown deepened. "No."

'Sometimes people dream of a fantasy so fiercely, it becomes reality,' Ignis said. *'She lived half her life in isolation, under the thumb of a ruthless father who was known to wield dark magic to torture and kill. Her entire family was murdered for being Unseelie, and that was all she knew about the outside world.'*

'All she knew, was the world hated her,' I said, *'like me.'*

"Well," Rory said with a sigh, "she's here now. You have an opportunity to ask anything you want, even the questions you weren't able to ask Gordan. That's a great place to begin, don't you think?"

"Yeah," I murmured, tightening my cloak around my shoulders. "I suppose you're right."

I was standing on the little balcony outside our room when Altrys returned.

The afternoon was clear, the sky blue without a wisp of cloud to be seen. I watched a hawk wheel around the slopes of the closest mountain, its wings spread out in a graceful arc as it coasted along the air currents. It reminded me of death and how the souls of the departed soared through the Greylands towards the next life.

Morbid, Elspeth, I thought. *Real morbid.* At least calling death the Greylands seemed less depressing.

In that moment, I wished I could become a bird—like Boone, or even shapeshift like Jaimie—and fly far, far away. But that would be selfish, and I didn't have it in me to run away. The old Elspeth would have made herself small, but the new Elspeth had become a warrior. *I even had the sword to prove it.*

Altrys leaned on the railing, his elbow pressing against mine. "What are you thinking?"

"You've been distant since leaving the capital," I said. "But so have I."

He sighed, his breath pluming in front of him. "I thought you would have been thinking about Aurae."

I looked away from the hawk and returned my gaze back to reality. "This has always been bigger than me and my mother."

"We don't have to go after the Chimera alone," he reminded me. "We can wait for reinforcements from the capital."

"That will take weeks to get here and ignite a war along with them," I argued. "We have to go now or everything we fought for in Un Alari would have been for nothing."

Altrys tensed, his brow furrowing. He said

nothing, but he knew I was right, otherwise he wouldn't have been skirting around saying it.

"I understand what this means," I told him. "We both know what your boss, what's his name, ordered you to do. Niarisshia, too. I didn't have to hear it to get why it was so easy to convince her to let us come on our own."

Altrys would be the hero and unite the De'ashlide with the Shri'danann. Niarisshia's rule would be all but cemented, the Chimera would be gone, the alliance would stand with the Druids, and the *Liash li Ashli* would be dead. I would die as the enemy, no matter what, but it wasn't about the price, it was about the ending.

"Ilbryen," Altrys murmured and I looked at him. "That's the general's name."

"I want you to know that if it comes to that, I forgive you." One glance told me all I needed to know. He understood.

"Elspeth—"

I placed my finger on his lips to silence him. It was the only time I'd touched him so intimately since leaving Sil Astrad. Since the morning after…

Altrys sighed and curled his hand around my wrist. "I'm afraid for you," he told me. "Something I should not be as a *shr'lei*."

"Something you haven't felt since Adrielle," I muttered. "And look how that turned out."

His brow furrowed. "It's not an easy choice, Elspeth. I don't want to… I…"

"Maybe it's best we stop whatever this is between us." My voice wavered and I looked away, staring out across Lir Cael.

Rory was right. I was becoming angrier the longer we were here. Was it my de Leiran blood outing? If so, did it mean I was destined to turn no matter what?

I hoped it wasn't true. I hoped… I hoped Altrys didn't have to go through with killing me because he'd have to live with it the rest of his life, so would Rory and Ignis.

To come so far and have it end that way was a slap in the face, but maybe there was no averting the prophecy. Maybe I was right when I'd selfishly thought about making a last stand against the Chimera. Maybe that's how I was going to break the prophecy.

In order to give the Fae enough hope to build a better world, I'd have to sacrifice myself.

"I'm okay with it," I said, straightening. "If you need to, it's okay."

Altrys caught me around the waist and pulled me against his chest. "I don't want to."

"I know you don't," I whispered, my heart thrumming in my chest. "But I want you to have a life after the black sun. Rory and Ignis, too. I don't want you to regret anything."

"Walking away from how you make me feel will be part of that regret, Elspeth."

I shook my head, lowering my gaze from his silver

eyes. "Better to break your heart now rather than later."

"It may not even come to that."

"But if it does… I want us all to understand what needs to be done. I don't want anyone to hesitate." I grasped his face in my hands. "Promise me, Altrys."

"You know I cannot lie," he rasped. "Don't make me."

"*Promise me.*"

"No."

"My life is not worth the death of your world," I hissed. "And it's not worth yours. Can't you see?" I let him go and wiped my tears. "I'm becoming angry and reckless. I'm…"

Altrys's expression slammed closed and he studied me for what felt like an entirety.

Finally, he nodded. "I promise to do right by you, Elspeth. No more, no less."

"That's not what I asked…"

"But it's all I am willing to give."

My eyes filled with frustrated tears and I turned away, my gaze finding the hawk still wheeling in the cloudless sky.

All Altrys was willing to give was *everything*. I just hoped it didn't cost him his life.

I froze as I suddenly understood why the elementals had pleaded with me to save him. My fingers curled around the wooden balustrade and I wished I could become that bird after all.

14

T hat night, Ignis delivered a message to Aurae.

'If you were truthful, meet us on the northern road three hours after midnight.'

I worried for him, travelling alone through the wilderness, but the cat could look after himself. It didn't stop me from fretting, even though he was the only one of us who could meet Aurae unseen. No one would look twice at a tabby cat slinking through the streets, and he would become invisible in the forest. That's if he took the liner approach. Ignis had a habit of appearing out of thin air when the mood struck him. I still didn't know how he did it and he wasn't forthcoming.

When he returned, we were ready to depart but waited for the inn to quieten before we made our move. Sleep was hard to come by, and none of us could manage to nap for even an hour.

'*The message has been delivered,*' Ignis said, leaping up onto the bed.

'*And?*' I asked.

'*She will come.*'

"Good," Rory stated. "We need a guide."

Altrys look up from his map and raised his eyebrows. "The mountain trails aren't marked."

The Druid rolled his eyes. "Like I said… we need a guide."

I looked at Ignis and shrugged.

'*They're on edge,*' he told me.

'*And you're not?*'

'*I'm a cat.*' His haughty tone translated surprisingly well via thought patterns.

I snorted. '*What's that supposed to mean?*'

"Do we need anything else?" I asked, when Ignis didn't reply. "La'luin gave us clothes for the cold, but we didn't plan on trekking across glaciers."

"The clothes we have are fine," Altrys said, folding up his map. "We will be cold no matter what, but the frost won't be a problem."

Rory shot me a look. He wasn't completely onboard with going after the Chimera, let alone climbing the highest mountain in the world.

"We have our Colour if we need it," he said. "We evaded the Chimera for decades and didn't have to deprive ourselves. It's no different here."

When midnight came, we spirited down the back stairs of the inn and stole into the stables.

Retrieving our horses wasn't difficult. The

stablehand was asleep in a pile of hay, buried tightly in a bundle of furs, his snores echoing loudly through the stone building. How he could stand sleeping out here was anyone's guess, though I wasn't about to wake him up and ask.

We led our mounts outside, buckling the saddles in the shadow behind the inn. *Finally.* We mounted and worked our way around the outskirts of Lir Cael until we found the north road.

There was no movement in the sleepy village. No guards seemed to be posted anywhere, at least not on this side of the settlement.

No one was crazy enough to want to trek An Valran… except for us. And the fact we were going to Si Ithqua at all had my toes already numb with phantom frostbite, no matter how much faith Altrys had in La'luin's magic socks.

I placed my gloved hand on Ignis's bag, hoping he was safe and warm inside. La'luin was found of the silly cat and her gift was thoughtful, but I doubted he felt the cold being made out of prisms and all. Perhaps there was some connection between his human soul and his body, he'd been in it long enough.

As we ventured farther north, the forest gave way to a desolate stretch of shattered land.

"This whole area is full of ancient mines," Altrys told us, his voice low. "Stray off the path and you may find yourself at the bottom of an unstable hole."

"Reminds me of Australia," I murmured.

The Fae frowned. "Australia?"

"The country where I grew up," I replied. "The early days of colonisation were built on mining. Gold mostly, but opal as well. People just dug anywhere until the government brought in regulations."

"Opal? I don't know it, but perhaps it is called something different here."

"It's rare and difficult to find," Rory said before shushing us.

As we reached a rise in the road, the view opened ahead and below.

The mine tunnelled into the side of the hill, the entrance looking like an ominous black hole. Mullock heaps were dotted everywhere, all piled high with worthless stones and dirt left over from digging them out of the mountain.

Workers had already begun to descend into the earth for the day. The size of ants, they hurried along the road, the lamps they carried bobbing and glistening like fireflies in the icy air. Metal tracks, resembling railroads, ran down one side of the path and disappeared into the darkness—mine carts. I wondered how the process differed from that on Earth. The De'ashlide controlled the operation here, but maybe they had a little magical help through other means—objects and the like.

The mine was just one of a dozen like it, each bigger than the last. It was a wonder there was any mountains left to dig into.

Sighing, I turned my attention back to the road ahead. I wasn't here for the gold rush.

No sooner than I refocused, Altrys spotted movement ahead. He raised his fist and we slowed our already plodding pace.

Familiar magic reached out towards me and I sighed.

Aurae.

I pursed my lips, my feelings on her appearance conflicting big time. I wanted her to come so I could ask more questions about her life, yet I wished she'd stayed behind in her stone hovel to rot.

"It's her," I said to the others.

We continued along the road and reined in our horses as we came level to her and her mount—a hardy little mountain pony with a dense, curly, chestnut coat.

"Greetings," Aurae said from underneath the warmth of her hood.

"I'm glad you decided to accompany us," Altrys told her.

"I admire your courage," she said, glancing at me. "The mountain isn't to be trifled with, yet you would take on both dangers alone. I am impressed, *Shr'lei.*"

"We better get going," I said. Clicking my tongue, my horse moved away, his movement spurring on the others.

We rode in silence for the remainder of the day. Aurae and Altrys led the way as the road turned from stone, to gravel, to dirt, and finally, to little more than a game trail. The way didn't give much opportunity to discuss anything anyway. Forced into single file as we climbed in altitude was both a breathless and noisy thing to tackle, and no one had the energy, especially as we were meant to be stealthy about our Chimera hunt.

We made camp in the shadow of a massive boulder that night. Sheltered from the wind, Altrys made a fire while Rory and I checked the perimeter.

Nothing stirred. The landscape was almost white under the thick layer of snow—the glare during the day had been brutal. Trees poked their heads out of the drifts here and there, the rock formations looking more like icebergs than boulders.

"It's so still," Rory murmured as we stood together.

"How do you suppose the Chimera gets out of their stronghold?"

"Magic?"

I snorted. "Hilarious."

Rory smirked. "Hey, I was being serious."

"The altitude sucks," I said, drawing in a lengthy breath that didn't quite fill my lungs.

"I've never been this high. I think we're higher than Ben Nevis."

"Ben Nevis?"

He chuckled. "I forget you weren't in Scotland long before all this. Ben Nevis is the tallest peak in the UK. 1,345 metres above sea level." Looking towards the summit of Si Ithqua, he grimaced. "It's a wee bairn compared to this monster."

I nodded and looked over my shoulder to where

Aurae was unsaddling her pony. Uneasiness made my stomach clench and I sighed.

"Ask her," Rory said, following my gaze. "It'll keep eating you up otherwise."

"Yeah, it'll eat through my stomach lining."

"She's your mother," he reminded me. "She wants to care for you, so let her."

I had no witty comebacks for him, so I hopped off the boulder and walked towards my mother. This should be easy, right? I'd grown in her belly and she'd given birth to me. We should have some kind of unspoken bond, right? Honestly, I wasn't sure how it was meant to work. The easy relationship I had with Dad was absent with Aurae.

I lingered a few steps away. "Can I speak with you?"

"Of course." She looked up at the mountain, her silver gaze moving up the peak as she studied the outline. "It's a long climb to the peak without magic, but it gives us time."

"When I met the queen, she told me about you," I said, ignoring her pleasantries. "That's how I learned your name."

"I don't doubt Niarisshia," she replied with a smile. "She knows far more than she lets on, I'm sure."

I stroked the neck of her horse, my fingers rasping over its coarse coat. "She said she met you as a child, yet you didn't mention it."

"I did know Niarisshia," she admitted. "I only met

her a few times as a child while we lived at Lor As'tuann, then I was taken to our family home after your grandmother was killed."

A likely story.

Seeing my expression, she continued, "I wasn't allowed to attend court or lessons with other children in the library. I was kept apart at all times, so much so, that others began to suspect our apartments had a spirit lingering within the walls." Her gaze lowered. "When Gordan left with you and I went into hiding, I had to learn how to *be*. How to speak to others, how to survive, how to make my own money. I was old enough to become a mother, but I knew nothing of the real world. I forget myself sometimes, and I am sorry if I frightened you in any way."

"There's too much at stake to take things at face value," I told her. "I may not have grown up knowing the truth of who I am, but I learned fast. Trust doesn't come easy for me."

"Nor should it," she murmured. "Do not forget the Chimera ruined my life as much as yours. I want to see them put to an end not for myself, but for you."

I narrowed my eyes. "If you say so…"

Touch her, the black sun whispered. *Touch her, touch her, touch her and bring her to me.*

Scowling, I jerked my hands into my sleeves and hid them underneath my cloak.

Aurae gazed at me and murmured, "It's becoming difficult, isn't it?"

My glare deepened. "What?"

"Controlling the veil."

I snorted and bit my bottom lip to stop myself from pouting like a child.

"My grandmother was the same," she went on. "The magic didn't manifest in myself or my mother, but it was strong in her."

"What was her name?"

"My mother's name was Lyndis. My grandmother was Aravae."

I didn't say anything at first, and Aurae remained silent, letting me gather my pride, no doubt.

"What did she do?" I asked.

"She died long before I was born, but I remember my mother speaking of it," Aurae replied. "Aravae didn't fight. She gave into it."

My expression fell. "And then what?"

"She triggered the beginning of the civil war… and was assassinated in the aftermath."

"The de Lerians have quite the history of being arseholes, don't they?" I snorted. "How does one person start a world war?"

"She walked into Lor As'tuann and dragged the king into death, body and soul." Aurae lowered her gaze. "But our family was despised long before that."

No doubt. The king must have been Niarisshia's grandfather and her mother Aibell rose to power in the aftermath of the attack, ultimately uniting the Fae and bringing an end to the civil war. People kept calling it a civil war, due to the entire planet being under the rule of one government. That was globalisation at work, I supposed.

"So, what do I do?" I wondered. "Struggle and hope for the best?"

"I wish I could answer that," she said.

Turning away, I stroked my palm over the rump of my faithful grey horse and went and sat next to Altrys by the fire. Rory raised his eyebrows from where he sat with Ignis—who was curled up in the Druid's lap in his tabby form—and I nodded once.

"Tomorrow we make for the pass," Altrys said. "Is there anything we should be wary of, Aurae?"

She's followed me, wisely choosing to sit opposite.

"After we cross the pass, we will come to the glacier," she told him. "It is called An Ud Xashri."

"That's a mouthful," Rory said. "What does it mean?"

"The River of Bones."

The Druid gulped and held his hands out towards the fire. "Forget I asked."

Altrys chuckled. "It's not that dire, Druid. The first Fae to settle the mountains discovered a great many bones buried in the earth. They were carried through the glacier over millions of years and came ashore in the areas where precious metals were found. They say they once belonged to enormous beasts that roamed the world long before the Fae were born."

"Dinosaurs," I murmured. "Buried in the permafrost."

"Definitely dinosaurs," Rory agreed. "That makes me feel better about crossing the glacier tomorrow."

"What are dinosaurs?" Altrys asked.

"Well, have we got a story to tell you," Rory began, making himself comfortable. "In the land before time…"

15

We crossed the pass the next morning, ascending towards the peak with surprising speed. The clouds hovered low and the sky was still brilliantly blue. It was freezing, and the air was thin, but at least it wasn't snowing.

The moment we reached the top, my heart soared and sank all at once.

Jagged peaks, thick forests, and desolate rocky valleys stretched all the way to the horizon. An Valran wasn't just a mountain range, it was an entire continent's worth of impassable ice. If we continued north, we'd probably reach the pole.

"Do you see that?" Rory asked, pointing to the right of the road.

Across the valley was a sheer cliff that sliced into a ravine. Low, muddy, green shrubbery and grass covered the floor of the valley, except where the remains of an enormous avalanche tore through the middle of it. A river once flowed through here, but it was now dammed by rock, rubble, and thousands of dead trees brought down from the mountainside. A lake glistened past the blockage, enough of it visible to see the ice forming on the surface.

"That's one hell of an avalanche," I said. "Wouldn't want to be under that."

"Someone was," Rory replied. "There's ruins down there."

My skin prickled with the excitement of discovery and I craned my neck, searching out the remains of Fae habitation.

Half the cliff face was buried in the tumble of dirt and rock from the avalanche. From here, it didn't seem like much at all, like I could reach out and touch it, but I knew these mountains were thousands of feet above sea level. The distance was deceptive.

I shielded my eyes against the glare of the sun and squinted as the outline of ruined walls poked out from the snowdrifts. Now that I saw them, it was easy to follow the pattern and find more.

Other signs of past habitation were also carved into the cliff face—windows, doors, stairs, and pathways.

"Who would be crazy enough to build a city in a place like this?" I wondered.

"There's plenty enough reason when money is involved," Rory said, angling his horse to stand beside mine. "You only have to reach a wee bit with your Colour to understand why."

"*Rory.*"

"Just a drop of a drop." He nodded towards the city. "Try it."

Pursing my lips, I tugged my hood low to shield my eyes from the sun and loosened my iron grip from around my Colour. No sooner than I'd allowed a splinter to work itself free, than the entire Earth seemed to light up.

"See?" Rory asked. "There has to be trillions of pounds of precious stone and metals. Gold, silver, crystals… it's all there."

I glanced up at the scarred mountainside and grimaced. "Too bad the mountain came down onto of it."

"Maybe it's fortunate." He wheeled his horse around. "This world doesn't react well to people carving too much out of it."

Remembering the Relic, I shivered. Giving one last glance at the cliff, I urged my horse around and rejoined the others.

"These are the ruins of the original Lir Cael," Altrys said, staring down into the valley. "In all my life, I never thought I'd see it."

"We can spare a moment to rest if you would like to explore," Aurae said.

Altrys shook his head. "We shouldn't stray far from one another."

"The horses could do with a rest," I said, seeing the disappointment on the Fae's face. "There are some buildings not far from the road. It looks like they once came all the way up here."

"I studied a great deal of original maps from this area," Aurae told us. "A great river once wound its way through the valley and emptied into the land below the point where Lir Cael now stands. The vast lake dried up in a matter of months after the city was buried for the final time. Now, it is all farmland and forest."

"Nature always finds a way to correct itself," Rory mused.

Aurae nodded. "It does, indeed."

As I dismounted, I rubbed my palm over the soft snout of my grey horse. I wondered what we were going to do with them once we reached the glacier. Set them free? The way was becoming more treacherous the farther we ventured into the mountains.

Aurae and Ignis stayed with the horses as Altrys and I skidded down the embankment and ventured into the closest building. Rory walked down the road, scouting ahead, preferring to be alone than a third wheel.

Shadows clung to the corners of the stone structure, while streams of sunlight poured in through the open roof of the ruin. It was so quiet here, that a violent shiver ran down my spine.

Can you feel them? the voice whispered. *Can you, can you, can you?*

"Are you all right?" Altrys asked.

For a moment, I considered telling him about the voice, but decided against it. "Yes. It's just eerie here."

"Do you feel them?"

I raised my eyebrows. "Who?"

"The dead."

I pressed my palm against the stone wall and shrugged. "Not really. It was a long time ago. Maybe that's why I feel creeped out… Maybe I'm sensing an echo?"

We explored a little further, kicking over stones and losing for artefacts, but nothing remained. The place had been looted ten times over long before we were born.

"What are we going to do when we get there?" I asked, the thought coming out of nowhere.

"We have to get there alive first." He had a point. The journey might claim us before we even set eyes on the Chimera.

"How far is the glacier?"

"Aurae says its over the next rise."

"What about the horses?"

"We can lead them across, then up the plateau, but they cannot go much farther."

"So, we just leave them?" I felt uneasy about pushing the animals farther, even though it meant we could carry less supplies.

"They will find their way to pastures, Elspeth," he told me. "Don't fret over them. The horses of this world are hardy, intelligent creatures. They will know what to do."

A rumble rolled through the ground and I pressed my hand against the wall to steady myself.

I froze and glanced at Altrys. "What was that?"

"I don't know," he murmured, peering out of the door.

"Avalanche?"

He shook his head. "Nothing moves on the mountain."

A boom echoed through the valley, the sound bouncing off the cliff. Altrys hauled me into the doorway as a stone fell from the roof, smashing into the floor where I'd been standing a moment before.

I breathed hard, my heart hammering, and cursed in Gaelic.

"Have we trespassed? Like in the forest with the kai'ash?" I whispered as Altrys held me close. "Does someone still live here?"

A thump, followed by another, seemed to confirm it.

"Footsteps," Altrys whispered.

My eyes widened. "Who do they belong to?"

An earsplitting roar tore through the air and the building shuddered.

Altrys pressed a kiss onto my forehead, then said, "*Run.*"

I didn't dare look back as we sprinted for the road,

the unknown monster chasing us. It roared again and a boulder crashed beside us, showering our fleeing forms with muddy silt.

My boots slipped and I almost fell, but a hand reached out to me from above.

I grasped Aurae's wrist, and she mine, and she hauled me up onto the road.

"We need to escape," she told me, shoving the reins of my horse at me. "We cannot fight."

I wasn't about to complain.

There was no time to grab Ignis. The cat yowled and dove into Rory's arms, burying inside his shirt as the Druid leapt onto his horse.

"It's the bloody abominable snowman," he cried, staring at the monster lumbering behind us.

I whirled around, my gaze colliding with twelve-foot of flesh, bone, and white hair. It did look ape-like with a broad forehead, sharp teeth, and humanoid figure. What it also looked, was pissed off.

"The glacier," Aurae said, pointing to the rise. "We can lose it there."

There was no time to argue. If that thing caught us, we'd be crushed in an instant.

It slammed into the house Altrys and I had been in moments earlier, the collision sending the entire south face tumbling to the ground. Then it picked up the largest rock it could find and hurled it at us.

"Ride!" Altrys shouted as the rock flew through the air.

"*Ha!*" I cried as I kicked my heels into my horse's flank.

We shot forwards, my grip tight on the reins. I could feel the terror in the horse, and if my hold loosened, I'd be thrown off. I didn't know which end was worse—being tossed over a cliff or being squashed by a Fae Bigfoot.

We left the road, taking the shorter route towards the treacherous safety of the glacier. The horses galloped across the ancient riverbed, their hooves kicking up muddy silt.

The monster sped after us, its speed frighteningly impressive for such a lumbering hulk.

"Keep going!" Altrys cried.

We tore up the hill and back onto the road, keeping our heads down. Crossing the rise, we twisted and turned through a thick layer of forest, before breaking out into the open.

The glacier glistened before us, hidden under a fresh layer of snow, making a headlong gallop bad news. There was no telling what lay underneath.

Jerking on the reins, my horse skidded to a stop, the others doing the same behind me. Aurae brought up the rear, her mountain pony surprisingly fast and surefooted for such a little package.

"We can't ride on the ice," Altrys said, struggling to keep his mount calm. "We have to lead the horses on foot."

"With that thing chasing us?" Rory asked. "*You can't be serious.*"

"It's the only way."

"Unless we let them go," I said. "We'll move faster without them."

"They need to come with us," Aurae said. "They carry our food and supplies. Without them, we won't reach Si Ithqua."

The moment of hesitation was all it took for the monster to catch up with us. I looked around, seeing it approach through the forest, the trees swaying violently.

Leaping off my horse, I threw the reins over its head and dragged the terrified beast onto the ice.

My boots crunched on the snow, the glacier not far beneath. Here and there I spotted glimpses of bluish ice dotted with streaks of dark silt frozen inside the ancient river.

We made slow progress—the horses were too terrified to move faster than we could drag them.

Behind us, the monster had stopped at the edge of the ice. It breathed heavily, its breath vaporising in enormous plumes as its gaze followed us with an intelligence that made me think it was strategising the best way to cross.

Turned out, that was exactly what it was doing. It put one foot onto the glacier, then another. When nothing happened, the monster let out a roar and raced towards us.

The horses spooked, rearing and shrieking as the glacier jerked underfoot.

"Let them go!" Altrys shouted.

The ice lurched again as the enraged monster lumbered towards us, beating its fists on the glacier.

I loosened my grip and my reins tore from my hands, tearing a hole in my gloves. All four horses bolted, their hooves slipping and sliding.

The monster kept coming as a crack split the ice, the sound booming deep into the earth… The glacier split open, ice shattering with a deafening crash.

The horses skidded as the glacier shifted. The crevasse split open and they fell, shrieking in terror. We could do nothing as the ice swallowed them whole, and I stumbled as I felt their souls tear through the veil.

Animals had souls—of course, they did—but I never expected to feel their loss so deeply.

The monster bellowed, lost to its rage, and came after us. It leaped across the crevasse, only to fall short.

"Holy *cac*," Rory exclaimed as the beast collided with the ice and tumbled into the hole.

The blow made the glacier shudder and come apart, sending our group in different directions. Altrys was the farthest away, and he leapt over unstable ground, hopping over the ruined ice in an attempt to reach us.

Rory cried out as he slipped, his arms waving around for balance.

"Rory!" I shrieked, holding out my arm.

He reached, his fingers grazing mine, then the

earth heaved and tore us apart, sending him towards the edge.

"*Rory! Ignis!*"

Aurae grabbed my arm as the glacier crumbled and we phased.

I was still screaming for them as we landed in darkness. My breath caught as Aurae steadied me, and I whirled around. We were in a cave, an opening above sending a pinpoint of light into the bleakness.

"We have to go back for them!" I said, grasping her cloak. "We can't—"

The back of Aurae's hand slammed into my cheek and my head snapped to the side. The force of the blow made stars flash through my vision.

"*Be quiet,*" she hissed, her voice dripping with venom.

My expression fell as I tasted blood. "*You planned this.*" I lunged and reached for the veil… but nothing came.

Aurae shoved me, pushing me to my knees. "Be calm, Elspeth. It will all be over soon."

My legs throbbed and I retched, the loss of my magic leaving nothing but nausea in its wake.

"What's happening to me?" I rasped. "What have you done?"

"Your abilities have been bound," Aurae replied as she drew the sword from the scabbard on my back. "It's temporary, but a necessary precaution."

"Where are—" I bit my tongue as the horrifying truth slammed into me like a sledgehammer.

Betrayal.

"The monster…" I gasped. "You knew it was there."

"Things were becoming rather dull," she told me with a smirk, retrieving my knife. "I had to liven them up a bit. I was hoping for the *Shr'lei* to turn and fight but being swallowed by the An Ud Xashri was better than nothing. It is a shame about the Druid, but I don't require his power."

"Why?" I asked, my shoulders sinking. "I'm your daughter."

"Shh," Aurae murmured, retreating into the darkness. "All will become clear soon enough."

I lunged after her but slammed into rock instead. I felt my way along the wall, my fingers scratching at hard stone for almost half an hour until I realised there was no way out.

I looked up at the pinprick of light in the ceiling and fell to my knees, despair wrapping around my heart and strangling it.

No one knew where we were. We hadn't sent word to the capital. No one was coming. No one at all.

My mother had betrayed me to the Chimera and for what? Her freedom? *Bitch.*

I slammed my fist against the wall, desperately clawing inside myself for any shred of magic I could find.

But there was nothing.

I was without my powers, and Altrys, Rory, and Ignis might be dead. Our plan was in ruins and now nothing stood in the way of the prophecy. If anyone was meant to die, it was me and only me.

I curled up where I lay, cold seeping into my bones, and choked back a sob.

"You didn't feel them die," I whispered to the darkness. *"You didn't feel them die."*

16

———

I didn't know how long I huddled in the darkness, my fingers touching the shifting light on the stone floor of the cave.

I drifted in and out of sleep, the cold seeping into my aching bones. Exhaustion and agony took me, and I sobbed for my friends lost on the glacier. For my father. For all the Druids had lost. And for my mother's betrayal.

A sudden and loud thud jolted me awake, and my head jerked up.

The wall shimmered, revealing a door hidden by an illusion, and two black-armoured Chimera—a man and a woman—stepped into my prison. The indigo metal of their uniforms was forged into thousands of tight scales that clung to their bodies, their shoulders and upper arms capped with solid metal leaves. The darkness was only broken by the toxic green of the insignia stamped into the left breast

—an elaborate tree with a grand canopy and twisting roots, reminiscent of an ancient Celtic design.

Neither Chimera wore helmets, their long silver hair and matching eyes masking the horrifying ruined faces they carried underneath. Powerless, I couldn't see through their illusions, and I was almost glad I didn't have my magic.

The man wrenched me to my feet and forced a black bag over my head. The darkness was absolute as they hauled me out of the hole, my feet scrambling on the rock.

"Where are you taking me?" I demanded, my voice hoarse.

The Chimera said nothing, steering me on a path to the unknown. No doubt, they were taking me to their leader, the illusive Vulis.

If I could just grab hold of a sliver of magic, then I would kill them all. While I still had my own mind, I would fight. The moment I was out of here, I would search for Rory, Ignis, and Altrys.

I stopped struggling against the guards, vowing to take *any* opportunity, no matter how insignificant.

We turned several corners, and I was dragged up several flights of stairs before we reached our final destination.

The black hood was wrenched off my head and I gasped as the brightness of the room blinded me. I blinked furiously as my eyes adjusted, my arms still held behind my back by the male Chimera.

The first thing I made out was the massive tree in

the centre of the room. It dominated the space, the canopy reaching the domed roof. The roots were so overgrown and ancient, they'd broken apart the silver and blue mosaic floor. It was obviously the tree from the Chimera's sigil. They had to have something tangible to worship, right? Why not a gnarly magic tree in the middle of a mountain?

I blinked again, focusing on the figure standing in the centre with their back to me.

My expression fell as I realised it was my mother. No one else was present.

"Honoured," the female guard said, bowing low.

Aurae turned, her smile widening. "Elspeth, I'm so glad you could join me."

Aurae de Leiran was the Chimera leader. There was no Vulis.

My mother was the enemy.

My mother.

"Leave us," she commanded, waving her hand at the guards.

The man let me go, backing away with a bow. Joining the woman, their boots thudded on the mosaic as they left. There was no questioning, no hesitation, just blind obedience.

"Honoured?" I whispered.

"Tomorrow I might make them call me majesty," she murmured, smirking as if it was a cruel joke.

It was far from amusing. It simply confirmed my suspicion.

Aurae had created an army of fanatics, biding

them to her with magic and fear. They'd become so twisted they'd forgotten their true selves… and lost their true faces. They existed to fulfil a single-minded purpose—the prophecy. The Chimera were slaves controlled by Aurae.

How many had I killed? How many had Aurae stolen? My mind swirled with uncontrolled revelations as the woman beamed triumphantly in the shadow of her stupid tree.

She'd lied when she said the ability passed over her. Aurae could manipulate the veil and the judgement of the souls of the living, just like me. Except, while I was floundering in the dark, she'd had a lifetime to perfect her abilities.

But I had one thing she needed to complete her grand plan. The ability to bend space time, to open portals, to nurture the growth of a new world out of the literal ashes of the old one.

The blood of the Druids.

"This place is protected by ancient magic," Aurae said, gazing up at the tree. "A vast forest stands here in another world a mere breath away, but here its mirror lies within the mountain. This beauty…" She placed her palm against the trunk. "This beauty exists in two worlds, but there is only one tree."

I shivered, the cold seeping into my bones despite wearing my cloak, and said nothing.

She sighed as if she was pining for something she had lost. "Gordan… He could have visited them all if he chose. The power was in his blood. *His magic.*" She turned, her silver gaze meeting mine. "A chance meeting changed the course of our world forever."

"Liar," I whispered.

"It's not characteristic of the Fae, but I don't consider myself one," she told me. "If I am to be the queen of a new world, I have to remove all shackles of this one. You and I are the beginning of a new race of magic, Elspeth."

Liar, liar, liar… How could I have been so stupid?

I remembered the images I'd dragged out of Owen's mind all that time ago in Edinburgh. A ruined land, a castle carved into a mountain capped with snow, fire and brimstone, black-armoured creatures, a woman with green hair fleeing across a frozen lake, armies clashing on a field of red, an enormous snarled tree rising out of an ancient forest…

It was a lie hidden amongst truths.

Aurae was a prisoner held in Il Fir by her father, but she had turned it in her favour, becoming the mistress of her domain rather than become a mindless weapon. She ruled through illusion and fear, while all others were oblivious.

She *was* the Chimera, but there was one thing holding her back from completing her grand plan.

The black sun.

Gordan's arrival was an unexpected surprise, and her presence on the lake that night was no coincidence… none of it was.

She'd tricked him into loving her so she could bear a daughter, but he'd learned the truth in time to save my life. Yenris'del helped him escape with me, her efforts to stop the world falling into the hands of her mistress rewarded with exile on Earth. Exile that had starved her of magic and had driven her mad.

"No," I whispered. "*No, no, no.*"

Aurae beamed, basking in her triumph. We didn't have to say it to understand. We were now on the same page, the ruse laid bare for all to see.

"*Yes,*" she crooned. "When you drew your first breath, I knew you were fated for great things, Elspeth. You would change our world."

I remembered the memories I'd gleaned from my father's tears in his journal. The women he'd spoken to in the tower wasn't my mother. She might have been a false memory for all I knew.

They will covet her power for the rest of her life, she'd said, but Dad had never listened to her. He was too busy looking to me, vowing a lifetime of protection. Yenris'del had helped us escape into the night, but... If that woman was my mother, why didn't she go with us?

Because she wasn't there, my power hissed. *He took you from her. He stole you.*

He stole nothing, I thought fiercely. *My father saved me from you. He bound my powers to protect me from myself.*

I was born on the night of an eclipse in a tower on the edge of the world amongst ice and snow. The unknown woman had called the darkening moon, 'the black sun'. The silver night had become grey and black, an omen fit for a prophecy.

Why didn't you tell me, Dad?

"I couldn't have planned it better myself," Aurae said. "To be born on the night of the Black Eclipse that inspired a piece of poetry that would go on to shape a new world. *Born of ashes, dead in darkness, a soul who bridges the gap has the power to destroy Druid and Fae alike. When the black sun rises, death will choose the hand of fate.*"

Stupidity bred fear. People believed the prophecy because they either wanted it to be true or they feared it was. The Chimera believed, and the Fae did because they feared a coming apocalypse. Which kind of stupid was I?

"The prophecy was a lie..." I whispered, tears staining my dirty cheeks. Had she ever loved my father? "It was all a lie."

"A lie that brought you home to your family, Elspeth de Leiran. Together we will create a world free from pain, where all will be equal."

"Those of your *choosing*."

"Those who are evil, daughter. I will not allow their stain to follow us into the light."

"What you're doing is no better!" I cried. "You want me to murder millions of innocent people!"

"No, not murder... I want you to set them free. To cast them through the veil where their souls can be reborn into a new golden age."

"You're finishing what Aravae began, aren't you? It never began with the rise of the Chimera. It was the civil war, wasn't it?"

"My, you are clever." She clucked her tongue and stepped closer. "Aravae may have set the wheels in motion, but no one had the power or the mettle to finish it. Not even my father had the strength to do what was necessary, so I had to take matters into my own hands."

"Was it strength…" I snarled, "or did he have some morality after all?"

"*Enough.*" Her magic shook the room and I winced, waiting for a blow that never came.

"You played your part so well," I rasped. "You even fooled the *Shr'lei de Delei'an.*"

"I even fooled that abomination, Niarisshia. *The queen.*" She grasped my face and studied me, her silver gaze hard.

I fought against a devastating wave of despair that hung over my head, desperate to keep a clear head. My magic was bound, my weapons gone, but I had my mind. There was still hope, no matter how slim.

"I won't do it," I hissed. "I won't be broken by you."

"You will return to me, Elspeth," she murmured. "Even if I have to break your will through torment to do so. You will become who you were born to be."

I wrenched out of her grasp, her nails scoring my cheek. "*I will kill you first.*"

Aurae's lips curved into a malicious smile. "Spoken like a true de Leiran. You make me so proud, daughter. Soon these trifles will be a distant memory."

She turned and raised her hands towards the great tree. Even without my Colour I felt the fabric of the universe shudder. Aurae didn't intend to stop here. Whatever world this tree shared would be next, followed by Earth, then wherever the next portal opened.

"In three days, the Black Eclipse will rise over the peak of Si Ithqua," she declared. "A powerful celestial event marking the anniversary of your birth. Then, you will see I am not the enemy, Elspeth. Your power will flow into mine and together, we will give birth to a new dawn. I am the mother of the new world." She turned, her eyes ablaze with fury bordering on insanity. "I am the Goddess of Creation and all will bow before me."

"Or what?" I asked. "Or die?"

"*Yes*," she replied. "And you will be the vessel of death who takes them."

The despair I'd been flighting slammed into me and my knees buckled.

I wouldn't have a choice even if I did turn, because Aurae intended to use me as a conduit. Millions of souls would flow through me into the void, the toll taking my mind until I was an empty shell. Afterwards, I'd be nothing more than a battery to power her next mass extinction.

"How—" The words died in my throat. *How could she?*

She was insane, that's why.

Aurae de Lerian was completely *and utterly* insane.

17

I stared through the front window, my nose plastered to the glass as I watched the postie screech his motorbike to a halt outside our mailbox.

The silver reflective stripe on his yellow high-vis vest shone in the sunlight as he rifled through his bag.

A heavy body crashed onto the couch next to me, almost knocking me off my knees.

"Did I hear the postman?"

I glared at Dad, who merely laughed at my annoyance.

"What?" he asked. "It's not like the man is delivering a mail bomb, Els."

"No, just my ATAR score," I replied, my scowl deepening.

It was the time of year all year twelve students dreaded. A letter containing high school exam results were being delivered to thousands of students across Australia right now. Results that would determine what university and course I could apply to enroll in the following year.

I wanted a Bachelor of Science and Environmental Studies

degree so I could follow in my dad's footsteps. It was just me and him… and he was my hero—fighting bushfires, saving endangered species, helping communities harness nature.

All I needed was the right number printed on that A4 sheet of paper.

I looked back out the window as the postie shoved a letter into the mailbox, then revved his motorbike and zoomed down the footpath to the neighbour's house.

"Are you going out to get the mail or not?" Dad asked with a chuckle.

I pouted. "Fine."

"Don't pout like that, Els. It makes your mouth look like a cat's bum."

Despite my dread at the letter waiting for me outside, I laughed, ducking as Dad swatted at me with his big hand.

"I'm going, I'm going."

"Do you want me to come?"

I rolled my eyes. "I can walk to the letterbox on my own, you know."

Dad settled onto the couch and kicked his feet up onto the coffee table. "I'll be waiting right here." He nodded towards the front door. "Go get 'em, kid."

There was no putting it off. I went outside and down the path, lingering on the footpath. The sun beat down on my bare shoulders and I felt a bead of sweat roll down my spine.

Take a deep breath, Elspeth…

I opened the lid of the emerald green letterbox and stared at the white envelope. It was facing the right way up, so I could see my name and return address printed on the front.

I only needed a 66.7 to scrape my way in. Only 66.7…

Sighing, I picked up the letter and tore it open. What use was it hoping? I already knew I'd choked. I hadn't excelled in anything the entire six years in high school. I hadn't even tried.

Don't shine, don't draw attention; make yourself small, say nothing, do nothing. Then the bullies will forget you. They'll stop making your life a living hell.

Except, they didn't. It only made it worse, and now my entire life was about to blow up in my face.

I slipped the letter out of the envelope. I only needed 66.7…

Please.

The paper shook in my hands as I opened it.

52.5.

My eyes cracked open, the gloomy cave a universe away came into view.

Look what being small got you, Elspeth.

I had no destiny. I could be whoever I wanted to be. I didn't need a score on a bit of paper or a piece of bad poetry to determine who or what I could be.

Didn't I?

I'd slept, but for how long? The eclipse loomed, the time of reckoning inching closer and closer.

My body ached from the cold, my heart bleeding as the truth stabbed into me over and over.

My mother betrayed me. My mother, who I'd wanted to know my entire life, bore me only to use me as a weapon of mass destruction.

I'd spent most of my life oblivious and without magic, and now it was gone and I felt empty. I was small, just like I'd made myself all my life to avoid the bullies who'd tormented me.

Now I had nothing to fight Aurae.

No one was coming.

No one.

'Elspeth.'

A pair of eyes glowed in the shadows, reflecting in the silver of light falling through the hole in the ceiling.

'I found you.' The cat slunk towards me, his paws silent on the stone underfoot. *'I can always find you.'*

'Ignis?' I reached towards him, my fingers finding the tips of his whiskers in the dark.

'Elspeth, I am here.' His tongue rasped across my cheek. *'Wake up.'*

'How…?'

'I understand where my magic came from now.'

'You do?'

'The Druids can manipulate the fabric of the universe, but I was gifted a piece of it.'

I wrapped my arms around the tabby cat, but it wasn't fur my arms felt. It was smooth skin and the rasp of fabric. My eyes opened and I strained to see through the gloom.

'Do not be afraid,' he told me. *'La'luin's magic woke more in me than my voice.'*

My heart leapt as I saw the man laying beside me. He had piercing blue eyes, artfully styled blond hair, and a sharp, angled jaw. It was the man Ignis had shown me when we'd Spirit Walked together. The warrior with the sword who'd sacrificed himself to save a world.

'*Wrap your arms around me, Elspeth,*' he murmured. '*I will take you from this place.*'

I stared into his beautiful, blue, human eyes and wept.

And he took me from the mountain.

We landed in a pile of snow—me face first, and Ignis cannonballing into it in his tabby cat form. The man he'd been was gone, his prism reflecting off the ice as he yowled in alarm from deep inside the drift.

"*O mo chreach,*" I heard Rory exclaim. "It worked, it *actually worked.* I'll never call you a fleabag again."

"Rory?" I stumbled to my feet, wiping the snow away with the back of my sleeve.

"Elspeth! You're alive!"

I threw myself into his arms, breathing in his scent and feeling his warmth. "I thought you… I… I didn't feel you die, and I hoped… *Tha mi duilich.*"

"You're sorry? What on Earth for?"

"I didn't know," I pleaded, clutching the edges of his cloak. "I didn't, *I swear.*"

"Slow down," he said, pulling back. "We're okay."

"Altrys? Where is Altrys?"

Rory nodded over my shoulder and I spun. The *Shr'lei* had dove into the snowdrift after Ignis and now held the cat in his arms, brushing the ice off them both.

"I saw Aurae phase," Rory said before I could reach for the Fae. "At first, we hoped she'd just gotten you to safety, but when no one came for us, we kind of figured the Chimera must have found you both."

"No. They didn't find us then," I said, my anger rising.

When was it exactly? The moment we met in the *Ashlar an lor*? Or the moment I'd shown my face in Sil Astrad on Niarisshia's orders? I felt my magic pour into my hands and struggled to contain the rush of adrenalin the veil pulsed into me.

"Where is she?" Altrys asked. "Where is Aurae?"

'In the mountain,' Ignis stated, leaping from the Fae's arms.

Rory frowned. "They have her prisoner?"

"You don't understand," I hissed. "Aurae de Leiran is a traitor. *She is the Chimera.*"

"But the prophecy—"

"The prophecy is bullshit, Rory!" I cried. "She made it all up to manipulate her mind-controlled followers! There is no black sun!"

They stared at me, equal parts confused and worried for my sanity.

"This is the same bullshit story that plagues every world time and time again," I raged. "No wonder the Druids wanted to seal their world off and never look back! The universe is mad! All anybody ever wants is power! And for what? So, they can feel good about tormenting other people? So they can suck everything that's good out of a world like filthy parasites before moving on? It's all a joke that means *nothing!*" A sob burst from between my lips and my knees crumpled. Landing in the snow, I buried my face against Ignis's furry neck and cried. "How many did I kill? How many? If I'd known... *I could have saved them.*"

'You did not know,' the cat told me. *'Do not blame yourself.'*

"The Chimera are innocents," I argued aloud. "They're slaves. They have families, *lives...*"

'Their loss is tragic, but you did what you needed to so you could live to stop Aurae once and for all. Now you know, do not let their deaths be in vain, Elspeth.'

"Innocent?" Rory asked. "What do you mean?"

"The curse never skipped Aurae." Altrys frowned and looked up at the Druid. "Their souls are controlled by her manifestation of the veil. They do not know what they do."

The Druid's expression fell, his horror clear. "*O mo chreach.*"

"Elspeth," Altrys said, kneeling before me, "I know you're tired and your heart is broken, but we need to know what happened. We still have time to stop her." I allowed him to help me up from the snow. "We've made a camp where you can warm yourself. Come."

They led me to a cliff a few dozen metres away from where Ignis and I had landed. A fire burned underneath a rocky outcrop that sheltered it from the wind and open sky.

Most of our belongings were gone, swallowed by the glacier along with the poor horses, but we had our cloaks, La'luin's socks, and each other. My sword, the gift Altrys had given me back in Sil Astrad, and the knife Rory had given me back in Edinburgh, were both gone, taken by the Chimera.

It took me a while to gather my thoughts. The sudden return of my magic had thrown my equilibrium off edge, the sensation feeling a lot like vertigo.

When I was ready, I told them everything. About the moment Aurae had phased me into the cave, the tree between worlds, the monster that chased us onto the glacier, my bound powers, and the painful truth of my birth.

How Aurae had manipulated an entire world into believing a false prophecy.

How I was to become a mindless vessel of destruction.

How tonight was the night her plan was to come to fruition the moment the moon was plunged into darkness.

How every soul in this world was going to cross the veil *tonight*.

"It happens every year," Altrys murmured. "The Black Eclipse. A fitting name."

"That means…" Rory glanced at me.

'It's your birthday, Elspeth,' Ignis said.

"How long was I gone?" I asked, ignoring them. I'd never celebrate my birthday ever again.

"Several days," Rory revealed. "It's hard to tell with the whole trapped inside a glacier thing."

"Days?" I swallowed hard and looked to the horizon across the valley below. The sun was already setting in the west, the snow tinting a brilliant burnt orange as it lowered.

"Elspeth?" Rory placed his hand on my knee, and I snapped back into reality.

"It's the eclipse. I have to go. I—"

"You have no weapons," Rory murmured, "we have no idea where the entrance to this castle is, or a plan to face another black sun. The very least we can do is make sure we have our strength."

"The eclipse won't begin for hours," Altrys said. "I know you plan to phase, Elspeth. You saw the heart of the mountain and can travel to it now. Time won't matter."

I blinked. "The heart of the mountain? Like the forest?"

"A place where the space between two worlds are at their thinnest," Rory declared, his eyes widening. "I understand now. That's how the Relic came here."

Now wasn't the time to debate the Darklands or the Relic. Instead, I diverted the conversation. "How did you get off the glacier?"

"Altrys reached me before I fell," Rory replied. "We both knew we weren't getting off before it caved in, so we went inside it."

I raised my eyebrows and looked at Altrys, who simply shrugged like it was an everyday occurrence.

"We rode an iceberg into the crevasse like a surfboard," Rory went on. "You should have seen it. Under different circumstances, of course."

"Ignis would have hated it."

"Oh, he *loathed it*," Rory said. "But we managed to find a way out. We tried to find the castle ourselves, but Ignis spouted some crazy theory about knowing where you were and just disappeared. And here we are."

"What happened to the monster?"

"Luckily for us, the fall killed it," Altrys replied.

'Did I mention I hate the snow?' Ignis quipped. He wriggled his way into my lap and nestled against my chest. It felt odd after seeing him as a human, but I cuddled him anyway. *'There is something else you haven't said.'*

"The longer I'm in this world, the stronger my Fae side becomes," I murmured. "You've all witnessed it ever since we left Sil Astrad. Soon, I will *want* to become what Aurae created me to become and everyone will die. If I want to hold onto the light and save this world, then I have to end it now. If I don't, then we will lose."

"You have the strength to fight against it," Rory said. "I've seen it, Elspeth."

I shook my head, my knowing guiding my mind to the truth. The same knowing that helped me find the Druids. The same knowing that made wielding

Colour so easy for me. It was the knowing of a true Druid. My father's blood spoke to me, and I would believe him over anything or anyone in a heartbeat, less than a heartbeat.

"I will go to her," I murmured. "Maybe not tonight, maybe not the next eclipse, but it will happen. I have to kill her while my will is still my own." My already broken heart shattered. "I have to kill my mother. I'm the only one who can."

"We are with you, Elspeth," Altrys said, taking knee in front of me.

"*Tha sinn còmhla riut gu deireadh,*" Rory murmured in Gaelic. "We are with you until the end."

"No," I snapped. "I have to do this on my own."

Altrys shook his head, his understanding clear. "Elspeth, no…"

"If I force my back sun to rise, then I can take her out," I said. "I can end it all before war sweeps across the entire world. The explosion will be a tiny blip on the horizon, and no one will be the wiser. No one will have to suffer."

"*But you will.*"

"She's my mother!" I cried. "She never loved me. She manipulated my father into loving her so she could create a weapon. I'm a *thing* to her. A thing she wants to use to murder billions of people. My life is nothing compared to that. *One life for billions.*"

Both men lowered their gazes as Ignis rubbed his head against my chin in an attempt to soothe me.

"It has to be this way," I said. "I'm a Spirit Walker. The black sun—*the veil*—will answer me."

"She will fight you," Altrys warned. "Aurae can break your hold on the veil and still turn you."

"Aurae may control the way between this world and death," I said, my resolve hardening, "but she can't walk in it. The veil will answer to me. My blood demands it."

This destiny was far better than the one she'd written for me. This one, I could choose.

"You were both right," I murmured, gazing into the fire. "Prophecies are just words after all."

I would drown her body in the river of death. I would shatter her soul and make sure no one was there to piece it back together. I would make sure the current washed every last bit of her down the drain until she was erased from space and time. There would be no next life for Aurae de Leiran, and if it cost me my own soul, then so be it.

I would never be small again.

18

————

I stood on the edge of the cliff, watching the full moon blaze silver in the cloudless sky.

Sil Astrad loomed dark and menacing, the danger waiting within clawing at my magic. Waiting so wasn't my strong suit.

Rory moved beside me, the Druid wiping at his eyes.

"Are you crying?" I asked, rolling my eyes.

"*No*," he replied with a pout.

I was past explaining my choice, so we merely stood together, watching the moon.

"Tell Delilah and the Druids that I'm sorry," I said after a moment. "Tell them that I wished we had more time."

"You'll get to tell them yourself."

"Tell them I love them all, will you?"

Rory sighed, his breath vaporising. "Even Vanora?"

"Especially Vanora."

We laughed as Ignis joined us in his tiger form. I scratched behind his ears as the big cat leaned against me.

"And you," I murmured, "look after Rory. Someone has to be there to stop him from accidentally opening portals to hell dimensions."

"It was only that one time," the Druid complained, holding his index finger up. "*One time.*"

I chuckled and wrapped my arms around his middle. "One thank you will never be enough for all the things you've done for me."

"Stop it," he complained drawing me close. "Or I will cry for real."

Footsteps crunched on the snow behind us and Rory drew back as Altrys approached.

The Druid coughed nervously and backed away, tugging at Ignis. "We'll give you two a moment."

Altrys took his place, standing close enough that we touched. His warmth spread through me and my heat leapt.

"I'm sorry I lost your gift," I murmured. "They took my weapons in the mountain."

"It was just a sword."

"It wasn't *just a sword.*" I cleared my throat and recited the script that had woven down the blade. "*Ashlar an lor, shride lei an val'ash.*" Honour the dead, for they give us life. "How did I do?"

Altrys smiled and offered me a shrug. "Almost. Your accent needs a little work."

"The one time I hoped a Fae would lie," I said with a cluck of my tongue.

His grin faded as the reality of our last goodbye flooded back.

"Take my sword," Altrys said, reaching over his shoulder for the hilt.

I placed my hand on his arm. "No. I won't need weapons where I'm going. Only magic."

I wasn't going in there as the *Liash li Ashli*. I wasn't going as a warrior trained by the *Shr'lei de Delei'an*. I was going as just me, Elspeth Odhweine. Not even a thousand Chimera would stop me from confronting my mother. A sword wouldn't help me tonight.

"I don't believe this is goodbye," he told me.

"Consider it a just in case, then."

He cleared his throat. "You have taught me much, Elspeth. Thank you."

I thought of our time in Un Alari and smiled. "You taught me more."

"If we do not see one another again…" He took a deep breath and held my hands in his. "I vow to uphold the hope you have given this world. I will fight to unite the Fae and bring peace to their hearts. I vow it." He brought my fingers to his lips and sealed his words with a soft kiss.

"Don't be so dramatic," I told him. "I haven't done anything yet."

"Consider it a testament to the faith I have in you."

My cheeks heated and I looked away. "Altrys, there's something I need to tell you."

He squeezed my hand. "Yes?"

I told him about the elementals and how they'd appeared to me on the road when he was shot with those arrows. How they'd asked me to save his life.

We'd come all this way, and the meaning wasn't so clear anymore. Something old and powerful wanted the *Shr'lei* to live and now, as I prepared to leave, he deserved to know.

"*Ak'ande la,*" he murmured.

"I came to think it was because of the orders Niarisshia gave you, but now I'm not so sure. I think there's more waiting for you out there, Altrys. A lot more."

"Time will tell… for the both of us."

Above, a sliver of darkness began to creep across the moon. The Black Eclipse was here.

"Rory. Ignis," I beckoned them close.

Ignis sat beside me, his tiger shape sparkling like ice crystals as the magic of the eclipse began to hit the stratosphere. As we looked up at it together, a curtain of green and blue shimmered into existence and lit up the night sky.

"An aurora," Rory murmured, taking his place beside Ignis.

'*A moment of beauty worth remembering,*' the tiger stated.

That, it was.

"Thank you," I said, standing before my friends.

"I wouldn't be who I am today without all of you. I won't let you down. Goo—"

"Don't say it," Rory interrupted.

"Okay, I won't." I grinned and spread my arms wide. "See you on the other side, *mo chairde.*"

Then, I phased.

I appeared inside the mountain, my boots stepping lithely on the broken mosaic floor.

As expected, Aurae stood before the great tree with her back to me.

She'd donned black armour similar to the uniform her Chimera slaves wore, though hers was more elaborate and vicious. Her green hair flowed free, reaching down her back and almost to her waist. She wore a twisted crown of black obsidian thorns, each point tipped with emeralds.

"You dressed up for me," I drawled. "How thoughtful."

Chimera solders poured through the door and circled the room with their swords drawn, closing in a tight ring around us. Sightless black eyes stared at us, each Fae poised in a defensive position.

"I've been waiting for you, daughter," Aurae crooned, turning to face me. "I knew you would return."

"You think you know everything, don't you?" I snarled. "You think your plan is flawless."

"Because it is." She spread her arms wide, her armour tinkling as she moved. "My children are here to witness their goddess give birth to the new world they've prayed for. Tonight, their faith will be rewarded. Not many can say they were witness to creation."

"All I wanted was my mother," I said, flexing my fingers. "To know her, to hold her, to know I was cared for. I wanted your love, Aurae."

Her eyes darkened as she drew the veil towards me. "I have none to give."

"Fool me once, shame on me. Fool me twice…" I shook my head as my eyes began to blacken. "If you want me, you're going to have to fight."

"You cannot deny who you are, Elspeth. You carry my blood in your veins. You are a de Leiran. You are Unseelie. You were born for this moment."

Let me go, let me go, let me go, the voice screeched.

"I know you can hear it," Aurae said, striding towards me. "You hear the voice of the universe calling to you. *The voice of the stars*."

Her blackened hand shot out, grasping me around my neck. Aurae squeezed, her magic drawing mine out with barbed claws that dug into my mind.

It would be all over soon. All it would take was a second. Just one to decide the hand of fate.

My power burned as I reached for Aurae, my hand clawing around her neck. I desperately tried to sever the connection, but there was nothing I could do. The floodgates burst open and darkness bloomed around us, the mosaic floor turning to pits of bubbling tar.

The black sun was rising.

The veil began to tear, the souls of the living crying out as our combined power spread. Extinction was beginning, and in another breath, they would all flow through me.

"Yes!" Aurae cried, bearing down on me as the tar rose to our ankles. "Call them to you. *Ahleida da, anahlei. Ore di ah'anith an.*" Her grin widened, her back eyes shining in triumph. "*Ashlar an lor, shride lei an val'ash.*"

I never believed people when they spoke about their lives flashing before their eyes. Near-death experiences seemed like a foolish notion for someone who could walk through the currents of death and live to tell the tale. But in that moment, as I felt the presence of a billion souls reaching for me, I thought of my dad.

I believe in you, Els. What does a stilly number mean anyway? You can be anything you want, if you have enough courage. There is always another path. Life is a battle, and the only choice we get is how hard we're going to fight for what we believe in.

And what did I believe in?

"Hope," I cried, fighting against Aurae's hold. "*I believe in hope.*"

"There is no hope for the lost," she replied, her lips curling. The tar—my manifestation of the veil itself—had risen to our waists as the Chimera surrounding us scrambled for higher ground.

"There's no hope?" I asked with a sneer. "Are you insane? Of course, there's hope. You wanna see what it looks like?"

Before she could reply, I pushed against her with every ounce of strength I could muster and we landed in the tar.

I wrenched the veil over us as Aurae dragged in lungfuls of tar, drawing our bodies into death. The room turned grey and we surfaced in the currents, gasping for breath while still trying to choke the life from each other.

Above us, the great tree burst into life, its branches writhing like a billion snakes, each reaching their venomous fangs towards us.

My feet found solid ground and the tar retreated, sucking back into the veil with a sickening pop.

Aurae shrieked, her grip loosening around my neck. "*Ah'ila! Ak'ande lir!*"

"No one can hear you, *mother*," I rasped, digging my fingernails into her grey flesh. "Only true death can judge you now."

The tree shuddered and its heart burst through the ancient trunk, beating a deep, throbbing rhythm.

It was alive. The tree was alive. Now I got why she'd chosen this place. The corruption of ultimate power and the lure of secrets no mortal creature should behold had eaten Aurae alive.

"*No.*" She turned her fearful gaze onto the heart

and let me go, her crown slipping from her head. "We will both die!"

"*I don't care!*" I screamed, pouring all my magic into her. The fire seared through my veins, the force only intensifying. "As long as you're dead, *they will live.*"

My magic pulsed, Colour crystallising around me in vicious shards of grey, and I pushed with all my strength. We fell towards the dark heart of the tree, the branches snapping around us.

The prophecy was a lie, but in that moment, there was more truth in it than there ever had been.

Death chose the hand of fate, and the black sun finally dawned as the Black Eclipse reached its apex back in life.

Flame erupted in a colourless explosion, devouring our bodies. Trapped in death, it had nowhere else to go and nothing to consume but us. The currents of death rose in a towering torrent, dragging Aurae and me into the depths.

The roots of the great tree snagged at our bodies, holding them back as our souls tore free in a blaze of white fire.

And then, it was over.

There was no more.

19

———

My eyes eased open, finding warmth and light full of colour.

I sucked in a sharp breath, almost expecting to find my lungs full of the waters of death, but it was far from it. It was the air of life.

I pushed myself up and held my head as it began to throb, confusion clouding my senses.

"Hey, slow now," a familiar voice crooned.

My hair fell forwards in a strawberry blonde curtain and I began to shake.

"Rory, I…" I stared at my hair and sobbed.

"Your father saved you," he murmured, taking me in his arms. "You are a Druid, Elspeth. *Only* a Druid."

"That's the first thing you ever said to me."

"Was it? I'm pretty sure I told you not to fash yourself." Rory snorted and his chest rose and fell with a chuckle. "Right before you took a swing at me."

"A pathetic one."

"Aye, but I wouldn't want to be on the end of it now."

I swallowed a sob as tears streamed down my face. *What had I become?*

"Hey," Rory murmured. "You don't have your Fae magic, but you have your Colour."

"What?"

"Whatever happened to you, you came out the other side as a Druid."

There was a weary emptiness inside me where my magic used to be. I listened, but all I heard was silence. There was no voice or heightened senses that told me people were around.

"I'm a Druid?" I murmured.

"One hundred percent."

I shook my head, trying to clear the haze. "After I left… what happened?"

"After the mountain began to shake, we didn't think waiting was the best idea." Rory hesitated a moment, then lowered his gaze. "It was a close call. Altrys and I, we both collapsed on the mountainside in agony. It was our souls."

"I know," I whispered. "That's when I… I pulled Aurae into death to stop her from using me."

Rory paused, his brow furrowed. "It was close, huh?"

I nodded. "What next?"

"When we could move again, we came into the castle to find the Chimera, well… not Chimera anymore. Ignis found you lying under the tree, soaking wet."

I swallowed hard. The currents had brought me back, or was its something else that resided in death? The tree was more than a tree.

"You were alone, obviously," Rory went on, "but unconscious. We brought you here, kept you warm, and hoped for the best." He paused a moment. "What happened to Aurae?"

"The heart of the mountain," I whispered. "It devoured us both in death. The tree…"

"Spat you back out again, by the looks of it," Rory stated with raised eyebrows. "It mustn't have liked the taste of Druid. We're too vague and bitter."

"I think it has more to do with a certain pact," I whispered, suddenly understanding. "The one Merlin made."

"Merlin?"

"The Old Ones, Rory. The heart of the mountain is an Old One."

"The tree?"

I could see the look in his eyes. The one that said he wanted to find out what it knew about the Darklands.

"I don't think it's something that likes to be messed with," I warned him. "It's not human. It has no emotions." I told him what I'd seen in death—the blazing heart and the writhing snakes and how it hadn't discriminated between good and evil.

"Perhaps you're right," Rory murmured. "You

were right about a lot of things, Elspeth. *Chan eil e ag obair. Tha mi duilich.*"

I pulled away, my heart thumping painfully in my chest.

Rory blinked. "What?"

"I-I can't… I can't understand you."

The Druid pulled a face. "Understand what? An apology? Elspeth, seriously? You've been trying to get me to understand my home will always be in Edinburgh."

"No," I said, grasping his flailing hands. "Gaelic. I can't understand Gaelic anymore."

"*O mo chreach,*" he exclaimed. "Your knowing—"

"Was Fae."

I took a deep breath and as my mind cleared, I felt it. *Colour.* I flexed my fingers and a spark of blue prism began to pool in my palm. Grinning, I looked up at Rory.

"How does it feel to be a plain, old Druid?" he asked.

I let the Colour absorb back into my skin and raked my fingers through my hair. No one was hunting me anymore, I wasn't feared for being Unseelie. I wasn't even a de Leiran anymore—the Old One had burned it all away. I was my father's daughter. I was simply Elspeth Odhweine, Druid.

"It feels pretty great."

'*Elspeth!*'

I looked up as Ignis bounded into the room as a tiger and dove through the air, his prisms morphing.

He landed on the bed as a tabby cat and climbed into my lap, purring and nuzzling as his tail flicked me in the face.

"Steady," I said, laughing.

Are you well? Are you really well?

'I am,' I told him.

My smile faded and I stroked my palm down Ignis's spine. Looking up at Rory, I asked, "Can we see them?"

The Druid glanced at the cat, who in turn, narrowed his eyes.

"C'mon," he said, handing me my boots. "Altrys is with them. He'll want to know you're awake."

Rory guided me through the bleak stone corridors of the castle within the mountain. The air was frigid, as if the mortar holding up the walls was made of ice.

Ignis had disappeared, keen to explore more of the structure. Apparently, this place was old. Like, *way old*. I guessed it would have had to be, taking the Old One into consideration.

"So, this is what the ice palace looks like," I mused as we wandered.

"I don't know how anyone can stand living inside an ice block," Rory replied. "I know a good rune to warm your fingers and toes. I can teach it to you if you want."

"I guess I need my nwyfre stele back, huh?"

Rory chuckled as we climbed some stairs. "You'll be back at Druid school before you know it."

I didn't want to think about what happened next. I was still coming to terms with what had brought me to this moment.

"Hey, Rory?"

He glanced at me. "Hmm?"

"You should probably warn everyone about the tree. It's sentient and—"

"Don't worry about it," he interrupted. "You just work on getting your strength back."

"I feel fine."

He knocked his shoulder against mine. "That's not what I meant."

I snorted as we emerged onto a balcony and as I looked over the edge, I gasped. When Aurae had said a thousand Chimera inhabited the stronghold under Si Ithqua, it hadn't quite clicked. Now, it did.

The hall below seemed to hold all of them, though it could have only been around a hundred or so. Voices murmured through the open space, the noise I would've expected from so many bodies, hushed. No wonder I hadn't heard them.

The Fae had set up a makeshift camp in the hall, having abandoned their Chimera dormitories. Their armour was gone and they all wore simple black and grey clothing.

"All these Fae?" I asked, my heart hurting.

"When we came into the castle, they were just sitting around, confused as hell," Rory told me.

"Their bodies seem to have returned to normal. Whatever magic Aurae used to bind them also turned them into those grey-skinned creatures."

"Do they remember?"

"The few I've spoken to seem to remember bits and pieces, flashes."

I stared down at the Fae, my throat tightening. Remembering my time in Edinburgh, my thoughts went to Owen. I'd killed him and knowing he was an innocent would follow me forever.

"What? Does your head still hurt?"

"No," I replied. "It's just… I can't help thinking about Owen. If I'd known, maybe I could've freed him and the others."

"But you didn't," Rory told me. "None of us did."

I said nothing.

"Altrys had been helping them adjust," he went on. "The truth hurt, but they will be okay in time."

"Where is he?"

Rory nodded up another set of stairs. Following his gaze, I saw Altrys talking to a male Fae—a Seelie with red hair drawn back into a messy man-bun—and when they were done, he turned. His gaze met mine and he grinned.

Practically galloping down the stairs, he came to meet us.

"Elspeth," he said, wrapping his arms around me. He whispered something in Fae and stroked his hand through my hair. "You've awoken. Are you well?"

"It seems I'm not like you anymore," I murmured. "I'm just a plain Druid now."

"No, not plain," he told me, pulling back. "*Never plain.*"

Rory coughed. "I have some… *things*… to do."

Altrys nodded as the Druid made a hasty exit and turned back to me, his silver eyes sparkling. But my smile faded.

When Ignis had taken me from the mountain and I'd found both men to be alive and well, it was Rory who I'd embraced. I hadn't even touched or kissed Altrys. Even now, I felt a shift between us, as if our paths had diverged.

"What happened?" he asked, making me wish he'd been there when I'd explained it all to Rory.

Still, I told him everything, revealing the truth about the tree and the Old Ones pact with the Druids. I could trust him, and it was the only way to explain what'd happened to my Fae blood.

When I was done, I leaned against the balustrade and looked over the room below. A fire was burning in a cavernous fireplace, the warmth dulling the cool blue of the stone walls. A Fae woman burst into the room, a bundle in her arms and threw what turned out to be Chimera banner into the flames. As the fabric ignited, a mighty cheer went up through the room.

For a moment, I smiled, their triumph infectious, but I was soon disheartened. The castle might be stocked with food and other supplies, but it was cold comfort. They had hope while I had regrets.

"What's wrong?" Altrys asked.

"Everything that's happened to them was because of Aurae. Because of my existence." I lowered my gaze. "I can't help but feel responsible for their suffering. The Druids, too."

"It was all her doing," he told me. "Now, they are well. They are cared for. They are free, Elspeth."

"Maybe, but I still killed Chimera. They were all innocent."

"Do not regret what you have done in service to our world, Elspeth," Altrys said, taking my hands in his. "A life taken by Fae hands before nature can claim its due is a sad thing, but do not despair what you did in ignorance. We all did things we wish we had not, but we were all deceived in equal measures. If there is blame to be had, it rests solely on Aurae de Leiran." He guided me towards the balcony. "Look. Because of what you did, because of your sacrifice, they get to go home to their families. They get their freedom back. It is no small thing."

I looked over the Fae and swallowed the lump in my throat. Seelie and Unseelie stood together, each comforting the other without prejudice. They'd shared something terrible, the scar binding their lives together for evermore.

Maybe this was the beginning of the unity the De'ashlide and the Shri'danann had hoped for.

Maybe it began here in the ashes of the Chimera. Maybe it began with Altrys.

"Now I understand why the elementals came to me," I murmured.

"This was all you, Elspeth."

I shook my head. "Freeing them was the easy part. What comes next will always be more difficult… and rewarding." Destruction took only a moment, but rebuilding took a lifetime. "Helping them return was always going to be your calling, Altrys. Remember what you vowed to me?"

He nodded. "I will fight to unite the Fae and bring peace to their hearts. *Ak'ande lei.*"

"The elementals saw it long before any of us." I wiped at a tear. "They need you, Altrys, *Shr'lei de Delei'an.*"

"And what about you?"

I turned to him, my list of goodbyes and rebirths so long I didn't know where to begin.

Altrys frowned and tucked a piece of my auburn hair behind my ear. "Your hair reminds me of the first rays of dawn," he murmured. "The light that brings the promise of a new day."

Ugh, why did he have to be such a romantic?

"Altrys…"

"I understand," he said, drawing back. "Everything has changed, and it is not a bad thing. Balance has returned to our world. Your sacrifice was rewarded with new life. A different life."

One where I was a Druid and he was a Fae, just

like my parents had been. He might not be able to have children, but it was an echo we both knew had ramifications… even for us.

I pushed away the truth so I could contemplate it another day and thought of something else to ask. "After all this time, I can't believe I never asked… What do you call your world?"

"Lor'Iyslar," he told me. "In your language, it means something similar to mother."

I smiled. *Mother Earth…* with a dose of added respect.

My resolve hardened and I knew what I had to do. There couldn't be any more delay.

"I have something to do before I can decide what comes next," I told him.

"What is it?"

I smiled, knowing I would be able to do it on my own this time. It wouldn't hurt to have the Elders and Jaimie and Vanora with me, but they would understand. Rory would be there, and Ignis, too.

"Will you help me?" I asked. "I have some people I'd like you to meet."

"Of course." Altrys nodded, his expression puzzled. "Anything for you, Lor'Odhweine."

I groaned. "We're not on that again, are we?"

"You saved our world, Lor'Odhweine, and you deserve all due respect."

"You're not Spirit Walking!"

I rolled my eyes as Rory flailed his arms in the air.

'Told you so,' I said to Ignis.

Altrys raised his eyebrows as we watched the Druid pace back and forth in front of the fireplace in the room we'd commandeered from the freed Fae. It'd been used as a command centre at one time—maps hung on the walls and even the table was carved into the shape of the continent we'd been adventuring across.

I played with a stone figurine of a tree—a symbol used for the Chimera locations—and sighed. There were more Fae out in the world waking up from their enslavement. All of them would be alone, terrified, and confused. That included Mindel and the Chimera from Earth.

"It'll take five minutes to bring them back," I said. *"Seriously."*

'I will go with you,' Ignis said with a swish of his tiger's tail.

'No, you need to stay here this time. I have to do this alone.'

"You just woke up from a sleep so deep I thought you'd become a vegetable," Rory declared. "It can wait."

"No, it can't," I retorted. "I know you're only trying to look out for me, but I'm the only one here who can go into death. They'll be afraid, Rory. Can you imagine waking up after decades of mindless slavery only to find yourself in a colourless prison?"

"She's right," Altrys said. "We cannot leave them there."

"I couldn't save Owen and the others, and nothing I do will ever make up for the fact that I took their lives, but I *can* help Mindel and the Earth Chimera."

Rory frowned.

"I need to do this." I turned and called on my Colour. "I'll be back in two minutes. That's down from the estimated five, FYI."

"What's FYI?" I heard Altrys ask as I summoned the veil.

I shivered as I stepped into death, the sensation of crossing a mere whisper compared to what I was used to. I wasn't as powerful now that my Fae magic was gone, but I didn't need it for where I was going. Colour helped me walk the currents, and it was what sealed the Fae inside their prison. The *Liash li Ashli* had no power here, she never did.

I felt out the anomaly, the time and place on the other side holding no meaning to where it existed alongside the living.

My Colour pulsed, the fold in the fabric of death unfolding like a flower bud.

I saw them, blinking at the sudden glare of light, holding up their arms to shield their eyes. Mindel was first to come forwards, his long, silver hair hanging limply against his gaunt face.

"Mindel," I said with a sigh. *"I'm so sorry…"*

He took a wary step towards me. "Who's there? Who comes?"

"Elspeth Odhweine comes." I held out my hand. "I'm here to take you home."

"Home?" he asked. "The only home I remember is my own world. It's been so long… If I have a choice, I choose death. I cannot go back." Mindel fell to his knees, the other Fae following suit.

"No, you won't be dying today," I told him. "None of you are."

He looked up at me, his silver eyes glistening with unshed tears.

"Take my hand. It's time to go *home*."

Mindel choked back a sob and reached for me, his fingers grasping mine. My Colour warmed, a thread reaching out to grasp Mindel's magic. My story, and the truth of what had transpired to the Chimera, flowed into him. It was easier than explaining it all for a third time.

His eyes winded in understanding, then he reached for the others. They all joined hands, linking together in one long chain, the truth spreading like wildfire amongst them.

"Are you ready?" I asked.

"Yes. We are ready."

"Hold on," I said as my Colour dissolved their prison and opened them up to death. "Follow me. It's not far."

The currents swelled as we stepped into them, but with my guidance, they receded and allowed us to pass. Bit by bit, colour bled into the world, the veil sighing as I emerged, a long chain of Fae taking their first breaths of life in months.

"*O mo chreach,*" Rory said, rushing forwards to help the disoriented Fae back into the world.

They poured into the little room, their shivering bodies quickly filling the space. Altrys guided them to other places and enlisted more Fae to help find them a warm place to rest and food to fill their aching bellies… all while they held hands, keeping the chain intact.

Once the last Fae appeared, I let go of my Colour and sank into a chair. Ignis sat beside me, leaning his chin on the arm, his blue eyes following my every movement.

"Elspeth Odhweine," Mindel said, bowing before me. "The magic of my homeland fills my heart. We can already feel strength returning to us. *Thank you.*"

"You are free, Mindel."

"You saved our world," he murmured. "You saved our souls from Aurae and the black sun."

He went to fall to his knees before me, but I leaned forwards and grasped his arm. "Do not bow before me. I am not her, do you understand?"

"You have given us a new dawn. A world to build in your image. We will forever honour you, Elspeth, *Liash li Ashli.*"

"No," I said with a shake of my head. "I am not a god. I am a mortal woman. Flesh and blood. I am no longer the *Liash li Ashli.* I come to you simply as Elspeth."

His silver eyes widened. "But—"

"All I have given you is hope, Mindel. What you do with it, is up to you. This next chapter is yours. Use it wisely."

Mindel bowed low, his silver eyes sparkling with reverence. *"A'ladrei,* Lor'Odhweine. *A'ladrei."* He backed away, joining his people, his role as their leader firmly in place. He'd taken responsibility for them and I was glad. It was Aurae's influence that had made him evil all along.

"Is it done?" Rory asked, kneeling beside me.

I nodded, my plain Druid bones aching after my Spirit Walk. "It's finished. I'm done." *I was done.*

Rory grinned and patted me on the knee. "So how does it feel to be a plain old Druid with limited battery life now?"

"Exhausting," I told him. "Utterly exhausting."

20

The sun beat down over Si Ithqua, the glare making the snow and the glacier below impossible to look at.

I turned my back on the view, smiling as Ignis bounded across the courtyard towards me. The tiger shook out his coat, the Fae around us stopping to stare as his prisms glittered in a rainbow of blue, purple, and green.

'*Show off,*' I drawled.

'*It makes them smile,*' the cat replied, and shook again.

It was a week after I'd woken and a whole ten days after the battle with Aurae, and finally we were leaving the mountain.

The Chimera, who now called themselves the Returned, had chosen a leader to come with us to Sil Astrad—he was Kymil, a blue-haired Unseelie with keen eyes and a way with words. The others would remain at Si Ithqua until they gathered their strength and received word from the capital. A small group would come as far as Lir Cael to gather supplies, while the rest of us would venture on.

Altrys was overseeing the preparations, busying himself with counting rations, while Rory chatted up some female Returned, treating them to his 'natural Scottish charm'.

Above the courtyard, the castle lay hidden inside the rock, and I looked up at it, wondering how deep it actually went. Not even Ignis had explored all the hidden nooks and crannies. The tree was a mystery, along with the people who'd built this place.

There were so many unknowns about the past, but the future was more pressing, at least for now.

'There are so many unanswered questions,' I said. *'For the Returned and the Druids. The Old Ones saved me... but who are they? What are they? Are we even supposed to know?'*

'Answers don't always come at once,' Ignis told me. *'Sometimes they come piece by piece.'*

Or heartbeat by heartbeat.

'I almost expected to wake and find you human,' I said. *'We never talked about that.'*

'The life I had before is over,' he replied. *'I was meant to leave it behind and find the next.'*

I snorted. *'You never counted on Delilah catching your soul before it could cross the veil.'*

'I didn't. But it simply means the next life wasn't as I'd expected.'

'I'll say.'

'Being a shapeshifting magic cat that isn't bound by basic biological needs has its perks.'

I laughed. *'I take it that means you like being a cat.'*

Ignis purred, *'Perhaps I'll learn more in time, too.'*

Sitting on the ruined wall, I smiled as a group of Returned passed by, their gazes lingering on me with shy interest as they went.

My ability to sense death, along with being able to manipulate the veil and my knowing, were gone, but more annoyingly was losing the power to phase. *Man, that was a handy skill to have.*

It didn't seem to matter. I was kind of looking forwards to being able to see the Fae world on our way back to the capital. This time, I would be able to enjoy it.

I spotted Altrys walking across the courtyard, holding a fabric-wrapped parcel in his hands.

"I have something for you," he said, coming to meet me.

"What is it?"

He unwrapped the parcel, revealing two blades. One the size of a knife and the other, a short sword.

"My swords!" I breathed deeply. "How?"

"They were found when we were searching the castle," he told me. "I thought you'd like them returned. Especially your Druid's knife."

"And especially my Fae sword." I held the scabbard close, the metal pommel pressing against my cheek. "Thank you, Altrys."

"Everything is back in its place. *Almost.*"

Almost. The word hung in the air, even though I'd thought about it often this last week.

"I need to go back to Earth, Altrys," I blurted. "I need to continue to learn what it means to be a Druid."

"Yes, I presumed so." He seemed to have put a great deal of thought into it, too. "Will I ever see you again?"

"Of course, you will. Druids are fond of exploring new worlds. *In a responsible manner.*"

He laughed.

"Rory's working on his portals," I added. "He thinks he can open one directly to the Warren. It's past time the Darkland Druid Elders met Niarisshia. There are so many things about this world that mirror our own, the path we have already traveled… and the places we were meant to go."

"You speak as if you are not… as if you are not Fae anymore."

"That's because I'm not, Altrys. The black sun burned it all away."

"By blood you're not. But spirit?"

We'd been skirting around this ever since I'd woken. Our understanding had been unspoken, but now someone had to bring it up. I was kind of glad it was Altrys. After everything I'd been through, I was still learning what it was to reach out to a world I'd made myself small to avoid.

"I will always be Fae in spirit and soul," I said, jumping off the wall. I landed before him and stepped close. "But this body, my blood, and my magic… they're not anymore. Honestly, I'm kind of glad. Being a de Leiran wasn't all it was cracked up to be." I opened my hand and a small crystal of Colour grew in my palm. "I am a Druid. That is all I am and can ever be from now on."

He lowered his gaze. "We're not the same anymore."

"We are. Not in the literal sense, but then again, I was never like anyone else." I used to be one of a kind.

"And now?"

I could see the hope in his eyes, and I wanted to feel it, too. "I will always love you, Altrys, but our paths—"

"Are taking us to different worlds."

"We have time," I murmured, embracing him. "It's a long walk back to Sil Astrad. The rest will come in time."

"The Druid?"

"Rory and I…" I sighed and drew back. "We're family, that's all."

"As long as you are happy, Elspeth, that's all that matters."

I shook my head and chuckled. "You're entitled to a little self-indulgence, Altrys. Take a little now and then, won't you?"

He didn't reply at first. He just smoothed a loose strand of my auburn hair behind my ear.

"Are you ready?" he finally asked. "If we leave now, we can reach Lir Cael by dark."

"Which one?" I asked.

Altrys smirked. "The old one, but I hear the last occupant moved out a few weeks ago."

"Oh, ha ha," I drawled. "Very funny." I handed him my sword. "Can you help me put this on?"

He took the scabbard from my frozen fingers and nodded. "Anything for you, Lor'Odhweine."

I met Rory on the road. Ignis prowled ahead, excited to explore the mountain trails now that they were free of house-sized Bigfoots.

We stood side by side, admiring the view of the endless peaks of An Valran, Si Ithqua finally at our backs. Far in the distance, the lowlands bled into the horizon. It was a welcome sight, knowing it was all downhill from here... *in a good way.*

"What now?" I mused. "I've been so focused on stopping the Chimera, the next part feels like a dream."

"We go back, Elspeth," Rory replied. "To our home. Screw the Darklands. We belong in Edinburgh."

"I thought you'd never agree."

"The Old Ones don't care about us. It's like you said—they're sentient beings, but they aren't human. They have no emotions."

My mouth dropped open. "You didn't!"

"I did." He held up his hand and pressed his forefinger to his thumb. "Just a little."

"And?"

"We've made something beautiful on Earth," he murmured, gazing down on An Ud Xashri. "The homeland is closed to us, but it's not our end. Our story doesn't end here."

So, it wasn't good news then. The Old One had confirmed what many of us suspected all along. The five families that had escaped the Darklands all those centuries ago were destined to become shadows, doomed to wander the crystalline world as guardians alongside the Relics. We were descendants of those who made the journey, and that made us party to their fate.

"We can't go back," I murmured. "The Darklands are forever closed."

Rory was silent as the last of the group travelling to Sil Astrad passed on the trail behind us.

"I told Altrys I was going back to Earth."

Rory turned. "You did?"

"I need to continue learning how to be a Druid. I missed out on a lot growing up human."

"So, you're coming back to the Warren?"

"I need a little structure in my life."

"What about..." He swallowed hard. "Things with Vanora... You and me."

I shook my head. "You're my family, Rory. It may

not have worked out like we planned, and our hearts…"

"Don't worry about me," Rory said. "I get it. What we share is more than love. It's not about that for us."

"What is it about?"

"I don't think there's a word for it," he said with a shrug, "but I feel it in my soul."

I grinned and basked in the warmth of the sun on my face. "And now we work to understand our place in the universe." And claim a slice of that hope I'd won for the Fae.

"It's like you said…" the Druid stated. "Home is where you make it."

"And who you make it with."

I took his hand in mine and pulled him down the trail, finally beginning our next great adventure.

The end.

GLOSSARY

Scottish/Irish Gaelic:

please note: the Druids deliberately speak the language in a more formal and pieced together way than fluent Gaelic speakers normally would. This is due to their nomadic heritage spanning across multiple worlds.

- *O mo chreach* - good heavens / oh my goodness
- *air do shocair* - take it easy
- *Tha mi an dòchas gum bi tìde gu leòr againn* - I hope that we will have enough time
- *gealladh* - promise
- *dùin do ghob* - shut your mouth
- *cac* - shit
- *Tha mi duilich* - I'm sorry
- *tha sinn còmhla riut gu deireadh* - we are with you until the end
- *mo chairde* - my friends
- *Chan eil e ag obair* - it isn't working

Fae Terminology & Language:

- *Li'deshri* - Mistress (an administrative position of import in the Fae court)

- *A'ladrei* - thank you
- *Liash li Ashli* - roughly translates to 'goddess of death'
- *Shri'danann* - the Higher Fae. One of the elite races.
- *De'ashlide* - non-magic Fae.
- *Tuathade'shri* - Royal seal. Represented by the eight pointed silver star of Queen Niarisshia.
- *Shr'lei de Delei'an* - Blade of the Queen
- *Lor'andann* - ealdorman/mayor/lord
- *Za'adei* - a Fae insult considered highly offensive.
- *Ak'ande la* - save him
- *Kai'ash* - an ancient creature that roams the remotest Fae wildernesses. Known by the Druids as a 'Relic'.
- *Ah'ila* - attack
- *Deash* - quiet
- *Addrei* - stop
- *Ak'ande lir* - save me
- *Ak'ande lei* - save them

Places:

- Un Alari - the village capital of the Silver Mountains, situated in the Northern Reaches.

- Sil Astrad - the City of Stars. The Fae capital.
- Lor As'tuann - the Celestial Palace in Sil Astrad.
- Ad Valrah - the Iron Pinnacle.
- An Valran - the White Pinnacles.
- Lir Cael - the village capital of the White Pinnacles.
- Il Fir - the Pale Lake.
- Si Ithqua - the Mountain of Glass.
- An Ud Xashri - the River of Bones
- Lor'Iyslar - the name of the Fae world

People (Pronunciation Guide):

- Elion - Ee-leon
- Niarisshia - Ne-ar-iss-hia
- Altrys - Alt-rees
- La'luin - La-loo-in
- Ilbryen - Ill-beh-ren
- Larel - Lar-el
- Aurae - Aur-ay
- De Leiran - de Leer-an
- Odhweine - Od-h-ween
- Maerinn - May-rin
- Vulis - Vu-lis
- Lyndis - Linn-dis
- Aravae - Arra-vay

Phrases:

- *Ashlar an lor, shride lei an val'ash* - honour the dead, for they give us life.
- *Ahleida da, anahlei* - Forgive me, daughter
- Ore di ah'anith an - This is the only way

Miscellaneous:

- Nwyfre (*noo-iv-ruh*) Stele - A tool used by young Druids to help seal their prisms.

ABOUT NICOLE

Nicole R. Taylor is an Australian Urban Fantasy author.

She lives in the western suburbs of Melbourne dreaming up nail biting stories featuring sassy witches, duplicitous vampires, hunky shapeshifters, and devious monsters.

She likes chocolate, cat memes, and video games.

When she's not writing, she likes to think of what she's writing next.

Follow Nicole Online:

Website: www.nicolertaylorwrites.com
Facebook: facebook.com/nrtaylorwrites
Newsletter: www.nicolertaylorwrites.com/newsletter
Email: nicole.this.is@gmail.com

to land in the middle of a prophecy of destruction. Druids, witches, fae, and shapeshifters abound in this thrilling magical adventure!

Find out more at: NicoleRTaylorWrites.com
254

See what titles are FREE at: Nicole's Free Reads

9 781922 624048